Part One
May, 1187

In the kingdom of Jerusalem, the campaigning season begins – and everyone prepares for war with the Infidel.

Chapter 1

A big man in brown, sitting behind a table. Big hands. Big chest. Short and broad. Head like a rock, face scarred like a battleaxe. He looks up and sees – what's this? A *street urchin*? Whatever it is, it's trouble. Trouble advances cautiously.

'They said I should report to the Standard-Bearer.'

The big man nods.

'You can call me sir,' he says. (Voice like gravel rattling in a cast-iron pot.) He pulls out a quill pen. 'Name?' he says.

'Pagan.'

'Pagan what?'

'Pagan Kidrouk.'

'Pagan Kidrouk, *sir*.'

(Christ in a cream cheese sauce.)

'Pagan Kidrouk, sir.'

Scratch, scratch. He writes very slowly.

'Age?'

'Sixteen. Sir.'

'Born in?'

'Bethlehem.'

Rockhead looks up. The brain peeps out from behind the brawn.

'Don't worry, sir. It didn't happen in a stable.'

Clunk. Another jest falls flat on the ground.

'Rule number one, Kidrouk. In the Order of the Temple you speak only when you're spoken to.'

'Yes, sir.'

'Understand?'

'Yes, sir.'

Rockhead smells rich and rare, like a well-matured piece of cheese. No baths for the Templars. Hot water is for girls and porridge and other soft, wet things. If a Templar wants a bath he can go and stand in the rain. That's what God put it there for.

'And where did you come from, Kidrouk?' (The unspoken question: out of a slop bucket?) Rockhead is highly suspicious. You can see what he's thinking. Just look at this runt! Smells like the Infidel, and looks like a bedouin boy. Skin the colour of braised almonds. Built like a horsewhip. Black hair. Black eyes. What in the name of God is this Order coming to? We'll be recruiting stray dogs next.

'I'm a local, sir. I served in the Jerusalem garrison.'

'On?'

'The night watch. I patrolled the northern beat. Between the Postern of Lazarus and the Postern of Saint Magdalene.' 'You mean the Jewry quarter?'

'That's the one. Sir.'

'And why did you leave?'

'Well, sir . . . it was the jokes.'

Pause. Rockhead's brows roll together like gathering thunderclouds. But the storm doesn't break.

'It was the what?'

'It was the jokes, sir. In the guardroom. Not that I object to jokes *as such*. Some of my best friends are complete jokes. But I don't like leper jokes. Or dysentery jokes. Especially when I'm eating.'

Rockhead puts his pen down. Game's over.

'All right, Kidrouk. Let's settle this once and for all. You're rubbish. You wouldn't have got as far as that door if the Order wasn't desperate. In April we lost four score knights to a Moslem raiding party sent from Damascus. Then the King called his vassal knights to Acre for the spring campaign, which means half our order is on the coast. Meanwhile the pilgrims are pouring in, and we have to man the road forts. See this? This is a report from Jaffa. Another shipload just arrived from France. Three hundred pilgrims – all heading this way. So don't fool yourself. Someone of your age, your background . . . You're a last resort, understand?'

'Yes, sir.'

'And I'll be checking your credentials with the Master-Sergeant of the City Police.' He takes a deep, slow breath. Now, I'm in charge of all the Templar squires in this kingdom, and you're on contract as a squire. We're very short of squires just now, because squires are dispensable. Understand?'

'Yes, sir.' (I understand, all right.)

'Take a good look at me, because I'm the one who'll pay you at the end of your six months of service – and I'm also the one who'll take it out of your hide if you break the rules of this most holy Order. The rules are very simple. A Templar doesn't sit in idleness, wander aimlessly, or indulge in blasphemy or unrestrained amusement. Remember Templars are Monks of War, and should behave like the lion that lay down with the lamb *at all times*. Is that clear?'

'Yes, sir.'

'As a squire, your first duty is to your knight's armour. Your knight's armour is more important than your own life. If you damage or mislay a *single piece* of your knight's armour, I will personally damage or mislay a piece of you. And I mean that from the bottom of my heart.'

Heart? What heart? Rockhead glowers across the table. Face like a fort, eyes like arrowheads. Asking him where the latrines are would be like scaling a watchtower wall.

He pulls a sheet of parchment from the pile in front of him.

'Your equipment will consist of the following,' he says, and begins to read aloud. 'One quilted linen shirt stuffed with flax. One coat of chain mail. One iron hat. One standard issue sword. One standard issue shield. One tunic. One pair breeches. One pair boots. One cup. One spoon. One bowl. One dagger. One blanket. One palliasse. One horse. One set of harness. One saddle. And one knight.' He looks up. 'This equipment is *not yours*. It belongs to the Order. There is no excuse for losing any of this equipment either on or off the battlefield. It is your duty, as a squire, to keep your own and your knight's equipment spotless. Weapons will be inspected every day before the noon meal while you remain here at

headquarters. You will attend all daily prayers as well as your own chapter of squires every Tuesday and Thursday morning. Meals are served twice a day, and meat three times a week. Any questions?'

(Please, sir, when am I scheduled to pick my nose?)

'Visitors aren't allowed in these headquarters, are they? Sir.'

'No.

'So if I want to see someone, I have to do it in my time off?'

Rockhead snorts. A sneer cracks his left cheek open, displaying the jagged black fangs underneath. Fangs like the ruins of burnt-out sentinel boxes.

'You don't get time off, boy.' Gruffly. 'You get seven hours of sleep every night. That's all the time off you need. Now. I've assigned you to Lord Roland Roucy de Bram. Lord Roland comes from France, and he's been with us for five years. The only reason he's here at headquarters is because he's recovering from a wound he got last Christmas. That was at Safed, where the last squire died.' He flashes his fangs again. 'Lord Roland's last squire was disembowelled by the Infidel, and his guts were tied across the road to the fortress.'

Hip hip hooray.

'Sounds exciting.'

'Lord Roland,' Rockhead growls, 'is the noblest of souls and a godly man and a great fighter. He is a gift from our Lord, and his guidance is a blessing. I'm embarrassed to give you to him, but I don't have any choice. Obey him, cherish him, and follow his example in all things. Because if you don't...' (Dramatic pause.) '...you're going to wish the Infidel had disembowelled *you*.'

I'm beginning to wish that already. Maybe this wasn't such a good idea.

'Please, sir, is it possible – would you be able to pay me half my hire money in advance? Or even a quarter, perhaps?'

'No.'

'But after I've been here for six weeks, say, could you not –?'

'No.'

Son of a Saracen. Damn, damn, damn.

'Go out that door and turn left, and you'll find the Marshal's office. The Undermarshal's in there, and he'll fit you up with your equipment. Then come back here and I'll take you to meet Lord Roland. If he's available.'

(Maybe this knight, this Lord Roland, could push it through for me, somehow. Or maybe if I take a pledge to pay the Viscount back in six months time. When I get out of this place.)

'Well? Get *going!*' Voice like a whipcrack.

'Yes, sir!'

'And be quick about it!'

The room isn't big, so it doesn't take long to reach the door. But Rockhead waits until the last possible moment.

'Oh – and Kidrouk!'

'Yes, sir?'

'Templars wear beards. So grow one.'

Grow a *beard*? (Standing on the threshold, one foot suspended.) Where the hell am I going to get a *beard*? There's no beard concealed on *my* person.

'Of course, sir. At *once*.'

***

You couldn't shoot an arrow from one end of Templar headquarters to the other. It's as big as a village. Gardens on the roof, all laid out neatly around stone seats and rainwater cisterns and sheltered courtyards. You can see practically the whole of Jerusalem, from the western side. Rockhead takes a detour across the roof just to point out those places where squires aren't allowed. ('For spitting in Saint Antony's grotto, a two-day fast; for pissing in the southern cistern, a five-day fast and a week's confinement.') To the north, the golden dome of the Templum Domini. Blazing away like a second sun.

It's nice, all right, but it's not for godless mercenary garbage like yours truly. Rockhead's here to make sure of *that*. Looking down from the eastern wall, a very nice view of the Valley of Kidron. The valley where the Templars have their exercise field – and where all squires report for their daile dose of fresh air. Squires don't need roof gardens. If you've got time to admire the view from the roof, you've probably missed your combat training.

'The stables open onto the exercise field.' Rockhead leans out over the parapet. 'You can't see the entrance from up here. It's right underneath us.'

'The stables are under here?'

'The cloisters are under here, and beneath the cloisters come the stables. They are the greatest stables in the kingdom – probably the greatest in the world. That's why they're so heavily guarded. Some of the horses down there are worth a prince's ransom.'

Makes you wonder how much a load of their dung would fetch. Rockhead takes the route through the old cloister, moving like a hog in mud. Head down. Stride short

and quick. Shoulders hunched. Past the armoury and the kitchens ('strictly out of bounds'), skirting the chapter hall, down a long stone tube like a rathole, taking the stairs at a run. Finally, the stables. You can smell them coming. They're as high as the vaults of heaven, and twice as long as they are high. The horses stand in endless rows like saints on a church doorway. King Solomon *never* had stables like this.

'Half these horses are from the south of France,' says Rockhead. 'They're the best you can get. The Infidels would kill for such animals.'

Sounds as if he's just given birth to the lot. Who needs a wife when you've got a gelding? There are people everywhere – squires, sergeants, servants – all raking muck and brushing hocks and filling feed-bins like priests tending a hundred four-legged altars. Squires might be dispensable, but horses certainly aren't.

'You will be spending a lot of time down here.' Rockhead makes it sound like a punishment. 'Lord Roland is very strict about his horses.'

'Which one is his? Sir.'

'He has three. That's one of them over there. That's another. And *that* –' (A flourish.) '– *that* is Lord Roland.'

Lord Roland, son of Saint George. He looks like something off a stained-glass window. Tall as a tree, golden hair, wide shoulders, long nose, eyes as blue as the Virgin's mantle. He's wearing a white robe (spotless, of course) and a knife at his belt.

If he's as good as he looks, I'm in big trouble.

'With your indulgence, my lord…' Rockhead takes the plunge. I have appointed a new squire. From the city garrison. He might be suitable – I don't know. If not we can

always put him somewhere else . . .'

Saint George takes a good, long look. You can't tell what he's thinking – if he *is* thinking. His eyes are big and blank, and shaped like crescent moons.

'Thank you, sergeant.' A lilting accent; lazy vowels; soft voice. Rockhead seems relieved. Another job off his hands.

'I've put him in your quarters, my lord, but we can always shift him to the dormitories.'

'Thank you, sergeant. You can leave him with me.'

'Very well then. Excellent . . .'

Rockhead shuffles his feet a bit, nods at Saint George, and shoots off to bestow more joy and delight on other fortunate souls. (You can hear him barking orders as he wends his merry way to the exit.) Saint George ponders his next move. What now, I wonder? More questions or more rules?

'I am Lord Roland,' he finally remarks. 'Sergeant Tibald has neglected to tell me your name.'

'It's Pagan, my lord. Pagan Kidrouk.'

He absorbs that without a blink. No comment. Obviously the strong, silent type.

'This is Fennel, my battle mount.' He lays a hand on his horse. 'My palfrey is called Brest and my packhorse is Coppertail. Fennel is not your responsibility. The others will need your attention. They are without spite or anger – a joyful duty.'

Ah yes. The joyful duty of steaming manure. The joyful duty of a kick in the guts. I know it well, that joyful duty.

Saint George caresses the big, brown backside under his nose (just my luck to draw an animal lover) and looks up, deadpan.

'Tell me, Pagan – if you were confronting an armed man in battle, would you prefer it that he carried a shield and a Turkish mace, or a shield and a short sword?'

Oh great. Terrific. A theorist.

'Well . . . that would depend, really.'

'On what?'

'On where he came from.'

'I beg your pardon?'

'What I mean is, everyone *knows* that an Englishman couldn't scratch his backside with a Turkish mace, let alone aim it at me.'

Silence. Not a flicker. Face like marble, eyes like glass. Is this a man or a monument?

'It also depends on what I'm carrying myself, I suppose. And how big he is. And how far away . . .'

'Have you ever been wounded, Pagan? In a fight?'

'Yes, my lord.'

'Where?'

'You mean where was I hurt?'

'Yes.'

'Well – once I was hit on the ear by a flying kettle. That was in a street brawl near the Syrian Exchange –'

'No. I mean in close combat.'

'In close combat?' Sudden memory of that pig-faced Saxon – Heimrad? Conrad? – chopping down from nowhere. Knees giving way. No pain, at first. Just the impact, like a blow from something blunt and heavy.

And there was the taste, too: that bitter taste of bile in your mouth.

'I was wounded with a sword, once. Across the neck and shoulder.'

'Anywhere else?'

'Not really. Just the odd knee in the groin. Tavern stuff.'

'Come with me, Pagan.'

People nod respectfully as he passes, moving like a cat in his soft leather boots. Out of the stables, into the sunshine. There's a big barrel arch over the door, and a ramp leading down to the training field – which is all dust and loose gravel. Nothing grows around here. Too salty, I expect, from all the blood that's been spilled.

Saint George has collected a mule-goad on his way out. It's made of light wood wrapped in leather. About three handspans long.

'Here,' he says. 'Take it and go over there. There. A bit farther. Just there.' He stoops to pick up some stones. 'I want you to hold that in your hands,' he says, 'and hit whatever I throw at you. Because I'll be throwing quite hard. Do you understand? I want you to guard your body.'

Wham! So here I am, standing in a sea of dirt, with a big mad Templar lobbing rocks at my head. *Wham!* Like some kind of martyr. *Wham!* He throws like a catapult – like ten catapults – ouch! – like a *hailstorm*, in fact. Ouch! (Missed again.) I've said it before and I'll say it again, my guardian angel has a mean sense of humour.

'All right, Pagan, that's enough.' (I should damn well think so.) 'Do you see what your problem is?'

Wait – don't tell me. You are.

'No, my lord.'

'You were trained by a much taller man. Taller and heavier. He must have been as tall as I am. And he didn't train you properly.'

Figures.

'You fight like a tall man. You don't use your weight to your best advantage. You are so light – you should move around more. And you're holding your weapon too low.'

'So you don't want me, then.'

'I beg your pardon?'

'You're saying I should leave. Is that right?' (I mean, I can take a hint. Especially when it's small and solid and thrown in my direction as fast as an eight-legged rat.)

'No, Pagan.' Saint George shakes his head, slowly. 'That is *not* right. You should pay more attention. I am telling you that your technique could be improved. You must realise this yourself, I think. What kind of sword have you been working with? I don't suppose you've acquired one of your own.'

Oh yes, of course. A whole collection. And a dukedom in France, as well.

'No, my lord. Somehow I never got round to stealing one.'

On guard! Will he or won't he? He looks thoughtful, but nothing else. I'm beginning to wonder if he's deaf in one ear.

'Quite,' he says at last. 'Then I suspect you have been fighting with weapons that are much too heavy for you. Much too heavy, and poorly balanced. In fact I don't suppose you were ever given a choice, in the past.'

'Oh yes, my lord. Once I was given the choice between a Turkish sword with a missing quillon and a Frankish sword with a rusty blade.'

'Battlefield pickings.' He nods gravely, like someone

who's just had his worst fears confirmed. 'You will not find any of those here. All our swords are Saxon – Solingen and Passau. The best available. I'll check the weight myself, I think. Just to make certain.' He looks around; up at the sky, back down at me. Back down his long, long nose at the midget mercenary who can't even handle a man-sized sword.

'It's nearly nones,' he continues. 'I must go to chapel every afternoon for nones and vespers. Do you know what they are?'

'Yes, my lord.' (They're dead bloody boring, is what they are.) 'I grew up in a monastery, so I ought to know. They're prayer services.'

Almost on cue, the bells start to ring. Saint George doesn't notice. He's too busy absorbing this . . . this *revelation*. This horrible shock.

'You were in a *monastery*?' he says, with more emphasis than usual. (Squinting a bit, as if to get me in focus.)

'Charity child, my lord. Nothing special.'

'I see.' He puts out his hand for the mule-goad, in an absentminded sort of way. 'You are fortunate. Not many are blessed with such a spiritually nourishing start to life.'

Spiritually nourishing! That's a good one. The sound of bells, following us back to the cloisters while he outlines my daily schedule. Normally he'll be at prayer in the early morning and late afternoon. That's when I should groom the horses, clean equipment, polish harness, mend our clothes, air our blankets, empty our chamber-pots, sweep out our room etc. etc. etc. (The list goes on and on.) But today those jobs have already been completed. Perhaps I should spend an hour or so in prayer and meditation. Just to

'keep myself amused' until he collects me for the evening meal.

'Perhaps you should reflect on what you're doing here, and what it means to be a Templar,' he says. 'Then we can discuss your goals and expectations.'

'Yes, my lord. And yours too.'

'I beg your pardon?'

'The beard, for instance.' (Might as well clear it up at the outset.) 'Because I've been told that I have to grow a beard, my lord. And I might be able to squeeze out the odd hair, all right, but it won't be what you'd call a *healthy* growth. Not unless I add a few clippings from my head. And a fake beard will make people think I'm an Infidel spy.'

He lifts an eyebrow. (Major breakthrough!)

'How old are you, Pagan?'

'Sixteen, my lord.'

'Very well, then.' A gracious nod. 'In view of your tender years, you are excused facial hair.'

He turns on his heel, so quickly that you can't tell whether he's smiling or not.

Rockhead's face is like a map of the Battle of Antioch. Every scar tells a story. Some look like gorges; some like patches of shiny white silk; some like piss-holes in the sand. His left cheek looks like a corn field, all ploughed up into neat furrows. Every hole is clearly visible from a distance of thirty paces.

'*Right!*' His call to order, sharp as a shutter banging. 'Before we begin this chapter of squires, I have one or two announcements I want to make. Firstly – sunburn. Our

Brother Infirmarian, Brother Gavin, has reported an alarming increase in the number of sunburn cases reporting to the infirmary. *Brothers in Christ* – are we men, or are we Michaelmas daisies? Sunburn is not going to kill you. I, on the other hand, *will* kill you if you keep on wasting our Brother Infirmarian's precious time.

'Secondly – new arrivals. You should have noticed a couple of strangers in the ranks today. Stand up, Kidrouk and Fulcher.'

Twenty-two staring faces. Fulcher has freckles, no eyebrows and a bad case of sunburn.

'Kidrouk has been assigned to Lord Roland and Fulcher will be posted to Acre next week to replace Bongratia, who was recently expelled for unmentionable conduct involving a female.' (Replace the word 'female' with 'pile of dead maggots'. He spits it out like a sour grape.) 'The Scriptures tell us "by means of a whorish woman a man is brought to a piece of bread". This is absolutely true and don't you forget it. Sit down, Kidrouk and Fulcher.'

It's hot inside the chapter hall, and there aren't enough benches. Everyone's squeezed together – sticky with sweat – under a pall of buzzing flies. The windows are too high to look out of.

'Now, today's tactical talk is on the subject of brigands. First of all, does anyone *not* know what a brigand is? Excellent. Then we should make some progress.' Rockhead starts pacing back and forth, and the flies get the hell out of his way. (They know what's good for them.) 'One hundred years ago,' he continues, 'when Jerusalem was delivered from the hands of the Infidels and restored to Christ, the way was opened for many thousands of pilgrims

17

to visit the Holy Land. The road from the coast became littered with their corpses, as bands of brigands picked them off like insects.

'But then a small group of knights, led by the Order's founder Lord Hugh of Payens, set themselves the task of protecting these pilgrims, accompanying each one along the dangerous pilgrimage routes. Gradually the number of dedicated fighters increased, until they became an army big enough to defend the entire kingdom. Right now they *are* defending the kingdom. But protecting pilgrims from brigands has remained a vital part of our Order's sacred duty to this very day.'

Pause for effect. You can tell Rockhead's learned this bit off by heart. Suddenly he snaps back to life again.

'Some people might tell you that pilgrimage escort is a soft option. These people have boiled tripe for brains. Pilgrimage escort is hell on earth – and not because of the brigands. Pilgrims are called lambs of God for one very good reason: they're as silly as sheep. Do not, *at any time*, give *any* pilgrim the credit for any brains. To do so is the road to instant disaster.'

Hear, hear. Tell me something I didn't know. Pilgrims on street patrol – your very worst nightmare. Either you're picking their corpses off scrap-heaps (robbed and murdered) or hauling them out of the gutter (penniless and dead drunk). Even worse, the ones that *can* talk. 'You call yourself a Christian? . . . Do you know who I am? . . . Are you going to do something about this? . . .' God preserve us from the pious pilgrim.

Someone sneezes, and Rockhead glares. He would 'appreciate total concentration because of the important

nature of the subject', etc. etc. Looks like we're in for a long haul.

'Some brigands are just hungry peasants who throw stones,' he announces. 'Some follow caravans like wolves, preying on stragglers. Some come and go in the dead of night, leaving the odd corpse behind them. But they are rare. More common is the Infidel noble. He tends to wander through this kingdom on his way from Egypt to Damascus, and although he only travels in small groups, he is a *man to be feared* . . .'

The noble – a man to be feared. Is Saint George a man to be feared? He seems too good to be true. And he never seems to smile, which is a worry. (Beware the man without a sense of humour.) At first glance you'd think he was the slow, spiritual type with his head in the clouds. But then you realise he's not. So what is he? Why's he so hard to understand?

'. . . The other type of dangerous brigand is the one who works in a gang, with archers and tactics. These brigands are usually bedouin tribesmen. If they are, you should expect many fleeting attacks. And if you let them divide you, you're lost. *Never* – I repeat, *never* – chase a lone bedouin. Why? Because there's *no such thing* as a lone bedouin.'

It's hard to concentrate when you've risen two hours before the sun. That was Saint George's idea of a good time to start training. In a room as dark as a Syrian's moustache, I was supposed to dress and arm him in the time it takes to boil an egg.

But it's the middle of the night! I said.

It's not the middle of the night, he said. It's early morning. And it will often be early morning when you have to do this. Now concentrate.

It was hard to concentrate. Hard to remember. What was the arrangement, again? His chain mail hauberk was in one sack, and his mail leggings, and his mailed shoes, and his helm – no, his shoulder pieces – were in the other sack. Boots at his feet. Tunic under his head. His cloak doubles as an extra blanket. Where was the swordbelt? Swordbelt was on the right, helm and arming cap on the left. Didn't know where to start, of course. Not at that hour. And Saint George was dropping hints all over the place.

Think, Pagan. No, not the tunic. I wear my tunic *over* my hauberk.

Hauberk. Right. Hauberk –

Wrong. The leggings must go on before the hauberk. Oh.

And what comes before the leggings?

Urn . . . the legs?

The *boots* come first.

Boots. Of course, I said (trying to stuff his left leg into the right sleeve of his hauberk). You're going to have to wake up a lot faster than this, Pagan – his voice in the darkness – otherwise you won't be of any use before a battle.

The question is, do I want to be of use? Do I have any *choice*? I'm in trouble, all right. If only I had some money.

'. . . The thing to remember about brigands like this is that they'll pull their arrows out of corpses to use again.' (Rockhead's still soldiering on.) 'They're always short on supplies, so their first volley will almost certainly be their last. Use it as a signal. If your shields are up, they'll have lost their chief advantage – which of course is surprise – without gaining anything in return.

'Right. Any questions?'

No response. The audience is propping its eyelids open. A blanket of boredom has settled over the entire chapter hall.

Rockhead's bloodshot glare travels over our nodding heads. He scowls ferociously.

'So I take it you're all experts on the subject?' he snarls. 'You'll know exactly what to do when you're confronted by a band of armed brigands, will you?'

Well I certainly will. I'll run like hell.

'Good. Then perhaps you can answer a few questions. Kidrouk!' (Oh no.) 'What's the most dangerous kind of brigand?'

Christ in a cream cheese sauce.

'The *most* dangerous kind of brigand, sir?' (Stalling.)

'That's what I said.'

'Well, sir – the most dangerous kind of brigand is probably one that's still alive.'

General laughter. Rockhead's eyes narrow. He is not amused.

'Stand up, Kidrouk.' He barks it like a dog. 'Kidrouk thinks he's funny.' (Addressing the audience at large.) 'Kidrouk won't find it so funny when a brigand spears him in the guts. I'll think it's funny, though. It's always funny when a goddamn fool finds out he's not so smart after all.' Raising his voice. 'If Kidrouk lives through tomorrow it's because the Devil won't take him yet. That's right, Kidrouk – you're on pilgrimage escort tomorrow. See how far a sense of humour gets you on the road. Because I've yet to see a brigand die laughing.'

Well that's odd, pus-bag. Because I've yet to see a face as

funny as *yours*. If it was a building they would have knocked it down long ago.

What is it about me? Can somebody please explain? What is it that makes me the *instant* target of every iron-gutted, bladder-brained, loud-mouthed, crater-faced, knock-kneed, vicious, murdering, soulless, arrogant dough-head in the entire kingdom of Jerusalem?

Chapter 2

The Cattle Market's empty – not a pilgrim to be seen. Just a wide expanse of beaten earth divided into sheep pens. The sheep pens always confuse foreigners. Why call it a cattle market, they say, when there's nothing in it but sheep? Don't ask me, lady. I just live here.

The flocks don't arrive from out of town until after the city gates open, and the gates don't open until the bells ring at sunrise for the prime service. 'Deus qui est sanctorum something, something . . .' Memories of how cold it used to get, singing Latin hymns at prime.

It's going to be a hot day today, though. A real sizzler.

'My lord?'

'Yes, Pagan.'

'What happens if one of the pilgrims gets sunstroke? Do we keep on going or do some of us turn back?'

'Safety in numbers, Pagan. That is the rule.'

'But what happens if the pilgrim *dies* on us?'

'Then he is blessed among men, and will go straight to heaven. Do not concern yourself with these things. They are my responsibility.'

Saint George, mounted on his fine white palfrey like a statue carved from ivory and gold. A reassuring sight for the pilgrims. Sitting up there in his white battle tunic, red cross on his chest, gilded sword in his scabbard. The visual impact alone should send every brigand with half a brain bolting for the hills.

A Syrian Jacobite wanders into view, and starts sweeping up manure. Still no other sign of life.

'My lord?'

'Yes.'

'What happens if no one shows up?'

'Pagan, they have registered their names in advance. With the Templar Commander. Please don't concern yourself.'

'There's one.' Sergeant Gildoin points a calloused finger. He's a little, dried-up man like a roasted nut, very fast on his feet. Doesn't talk a lot. Big nose. Highly accurate when spitting. 'And there's another.'

'Where is the chaplain?' Saint George sounds worried. 'He is already late.'

The pilgrims are staggering along under a load of earthenware bottles. They look up, see us, wave. There are three of them: a man, a woman and a baby.

One of the sergeants crosses himself.

'Sergeant Bonetus!' (Saint George, measuring the distance between himself and the dreaded infant with

his eyes.) 'Where is Father Amiel? He should be here by now.'

'Yes, my lord.'

'Fetch him quickly. There are women coming.'

'Yes my lord.'

Bonetus disappears in a cloud of dust. More women are approaching. They wear big, shady hats, and carry bottles and figs and bread and wine, and rags for emergencies. Some ride donkeys, some lead mules. The one with the baby is fat and sunburned, and probably of Saxon stock.

'Ahoy there!' she cries. 'Are you going to the Jordan, good gentlemen?'

No response. The invisible escort, avoiding her eye. Looking around for the priest.

'Excuse me.' (She's not about to give up that easily.) 'We're going to the Jordan. Are *you* going to the Jordan?'

'Yes we are.' Gildoin, gruffly.

'Oh good. *Corba! Sweetheart! It's over here!*' A voice like the squeal of pigs in a slaughterhouse. 'I wasn't sure at first,' she continues, 'because they said to meet at the Cattle Market, and those look like *sheep* pens to me.' Fixing her bright little eyes on Gildoin, who glances in turn at Saint George. No help from that quarter. Templar knights aren't allowed to speak to the opposite sex.

But reinforcements are on the way.

'Can I help you, madam?' It's Father Amiel. 'Are you part of the Jordan pilgrimage?'

'Yes we are. This is my husband Radulf. Radulf Marti. And I'm Agnes. And this is my baby Gerald. We're from Piedmont.'

'One moment please.'

Father Amiel: just a wisp of skin and gristle, held together by clothes. You can practically see right through him. The roll of parchment in his hands looks sturdier than he does.

'Ah yes,' he quavers. 'You're marked down here. From the Venetian group tour?'

'That's right, Father. The rest are coming. But we've lost a few on the way. Poor old Master Cyprien broke his jaw yesterday in the Templar crypt chapel. God's vengeance, you know.'

(If they're not careful, that chaplain's going to disintegrate under the sheer force of her personality.)

'No.' A feeble murmur. 'I didn't know . . .'

'Haven't they told you? We were lined up to kiss the cradle of Christ and he tried to bite a bit off it! Can you believe that? For a souvenir! I told him – lovey, I said, there's no need to *steal*. You can buy a nice cheap saint's toenail on every street corner in Jerusalem. It's the religious relic capital of the world, I said. But he wouldn't listen.'

'Yes. I see. Thank you –'

'And then we lost someone on the ship, didn't we, Radulf? Died of seasickness.'

Died of *seasickness*? That I don't believe. You can't die of seasickness, sweetheart. No matter how much you might want to, when you have it. 'But that's impossible. He couldn't have died of seasickness. Nobody can.'

'Oh, but he did. He was vomiting over the side and he fell into the sea.'

'Pagan.' A quiet warning from Saint George. Squires should be seen and not heard, by the look of it. He stares off

into space as the pilgrims gather round to check their names off our list. A pretty frightening bunch. Four cripples, nine old men (one obviously senile), four children (three of them blind), a hairy fanatic in rags and bare feet, a sick-looking Cistercian monk, three able-bodied men and eighteen women (four of them nuns). Keeping this lot safe and sound is going to be a real challenge.

'Where are their donkeys, Father?' Saint George, the Good Shepherd. 'We seem to be missing at least four.'

But the chaplain's ears are otherwise engaged. There's a noisy foreigner rattling away at his elbow like the Tower of Babel. Don't recognise the language, myself. Sounds like a drunkard drowning in fish guts.

'*Father.*' Saint George raises his voice. 'Father, we *cannot* leave until everyone is mounted.'

'Look, my lord.'

Bonetus points. And there they are! A procession of donkeys moving our way, emerging from behind the awning which usually shelters the Royal Inspector of Weights and Balances. There's a man leading the procession. Even at this distance, it's obvious who he is.

Joscelin.

'That's our guide,' Agnes informs the world at large. 'That's our guide, and those are our donkeys.'

(Guide? *Guide?* If he's a guide, I'm Saint Lucy of Syracuse.)

Suddenly the bells start to ring.

'We must get moving.' Saint George makes his decision. No arguments, no delays. 'They will open the gates any moment. Father! Is everyone present who should be?'

'Yes, my lord.'

'Then I would like to make my announcement. As soon as possible, please.'

Watch your backs, everyone – Joscelin's joined the crowd. Dressed in white linen, hair trimmed, no jewellery, sensible walking boots, beasts of burden at his heels. I can't believe I'm seeing this. Some of the pilgrims surge towards him, eager to grab the best animals. Not that there's much of a choice, mind you. But as everyone knows, a pilgrim will saddle up anything with more than two legs that's going in approximately the right direction.

Joscelin looks up; spots me; stares; blinks; smiles. That's right, maggot-bag. Smile, why don't you? Smile while you still have the teeth to smile *with*.

'Yes, yes,' he chirrups, 'yes, yes, these are your donkeys. Yes, you can take your choice, Dame Agnes. This one is called Legless, that's Fang, that's Manure, that's Cretin, that's Corpse, and that's Apocalypse.'

Pause. Doubtful glances flash from pilgrim to pilgrim.

'Don't worry.' Joscelin's sweetest voice. 'Corpse isn't dead. He just stinks, that's all.'

A wolf in sheep's clothing. I can't believe I'm seeing this. He looks like a choirboy in that outfit. Like the Archangel Gabriel's maiden aunt. Last time I saw him . . . can't remember too well. Drunk, of course. In some appalling establishment. Lots of silk pillows, wool carpets, Persian pipes . . . a sick dog, somewhere. And a girl eating plums, spitting the stones at a fat, snoring ship-master who'd just done a deal with Joscelin. A two-year supply of dumb pilgrims – sea-dazzled pilgrims straight off the decks. Shepherded into Joscelin's arms for a small, regular fee.

And Joscelin indulging his passion for dates. Licking his sticky fingers with a viper's tongue. 'This is my old friend Pagan.' (Offering me the jug of wine.) 'We practically grew up together . . .'

'*Attention! Attention, please!*' Father Amiel claps his hands. 'Jordan pilgrims! Quiet for Lord Roland Roucy de Bram! Lord Roland wants to speak to you!'

Respectful silence. Nobody wants to compete with Saint George. Not even Joscelin, who's reserved 'Apocalypse' for himself. Everyone puts on that pious, sheepish expression – the look you see on people in church when they've just spent six months breaking all ten commandments plus a few more they've thought up themselves.

'God's pilgrims,' Saint George intones, 'on behalf of the Order of the Temple, I welcome you to Jerusalem. These ten soldiers in Christ – and myself, of course – will be your escort to the holy river of Jordan today. Usually the Order provides one Templar knight for every five pilgrims. Unfortunately, for the safety of this kingdom (which is currently threatened by the armies of that arch-Infidel Saladin) we cannot spare so many knights at this time. But the sergeants you see before you will serve as devoutly and courageously as any knight.'

Disappointment reigns. What, no aristocrats? (But I promised Auntie Maud . . .)

'There are only three rules governing this journey.' Saint George, ignoring the general reaction. 'The first is that we shall stop twice on our way to, and twice on our way from, the holy river. So anyone with dysentery or other stomach problems must forgo this trip. We cannot afford to stop too many times if we want to return before sunset.

'Secondly, there is a restriction on the number of holy-water bottles you can fill at the Jordan. From past experience we have found that any more than eight bottles *per pilgrim* will severely hamper our progress.'

Groans of dismay.

'I'm sorry if this will inconvenience you, but it's for your own safety. Now, the third and final rule is that when I tell you to do something, *you must do it*. If you don't, it will probably cost you your life.

'That is all I have to say, except that I hope you will all benefit from the holy river's healing waters and that you will join Father Amiel in a prayer before we leave.'

A spattering of applause, undercut by discontented murmurs. (Half the bottles will have to go. But what about Grandma? And what about Uncle Edmund? We have to bring some back for him, because of his skin ulcers . . .)

'Thank you, my lord.' Now it's Father Amiel's turn. 'I think Psalm Three would be appropriate. "Lord, how art they increased that trouble me! Many are they that rise up against me. But thou, O Lord, art a shield for me: my glory and the lifter up of mine head. I will not be afraid of ten thousands of people that have set themselves against me round about. Arise, O Lord; save me, O my God: for thou hast smitten all mine enemies upon the cheek bone; thou hast broken the teeth of the ungodly. Salvation belongeth to the Lord: thy blessing is upon thy people."'

Amen.

Still very early. Dew in the shadows, chill in the air, shepherds on the road heading for Jerusalem. *Their* flocks

are nervous and obedient. Not like ours. Ours is full of pious pea-heads who want to linger over every sacred sight. First stop: Bethany. Straggling village famous for a particularly nasty murder four years ago, when some miller was hacked to pieces and the limbs thrown around a pigsty. No mention of *that*, naturally. Joscelin pointing out notable features.

'On your right is the village of Bethany, at the foot of the Mount of Olives, which was the home of Lazarus and his sisters Mary and Martha. His crypt lies beneath that church, which is the Church of Lazarus. The other church is the Church of Saint Mary Magdalene. Bethany was also the home of Simon the Leper, where our Lord Jesus Christ lodged during Holy Week. If you look in the Church of Lazarus, you will see the broken alabaster box from the Gospel of Matthew. This box is known to have healed palsy and some convulsive ailments. The tower you see belongs to the convent of Queen Melisande, who was our queen here from 1131 until 1161 – a very holy woman who contributed greatly to the beauty of our sacred places.'

Christ in a cream cheese sauce.

'And that rock, Master Joscelin?' The nun with the frog's face. 'Will you tell us about that rock, please?'

'*That* rock?'

'Yes please.'

Can't believe his ears. But treads carefully, as usual. 'You want to know about that rock,' he repeats.

'Well look how it's cloven into three parts! One cleft in three, like the Holy Trinity! Surely it must be the scene of some miracle?'

Poor, stupid Frogface. Her bulging eyes are wet with emotion. People like Frogface think Jerusalem's streets are

paved with the bones of martyrs, and every sunbeam is solid gold. You can't help feeling sorry for them – especially with leeches like Joscelin around.

'Oh, *that* rock!' he says. 'Of course, Sister. That's where they buried the man who ate one of the swine that had devils in them, from the Gospel of Matthew chapter eight. He wouldn't lie down when he was dead, you see, so they had to roll that big rock on top of him. And God smote the rock to kill the devil. And that's why it's now in three parts.'

Gasps of amazement. But all lies, of course. Lies are Joscelin's stock in trade. The question is, should I tell someone? Should I tell Saint George that we're presently escorting a thief, blackmailer and notorious corrupter of women? Someone who cheats dumb pilgrims when they want to exchange their foreign money for local dinars? Someone who gets them drunk and pushes them into the arms of other thieves, so that they're left with nothing except the dirt under their fingernails?

I should, of course. But it might be awkward. It might cast a murky light on my own history. (Is that so, Pagan? And how do you come to know all this? And where did you *meet* this man? And how long have you been acquainted with him?)

They might throw me out of the Order. Which is a risk I can't take – not just now. Not when things are so difficult.

'Which saint am I?' Now Frogface has started a game of 'Saints'. Filling in time until the next sacred monument. 'My name begins with "A" –'

'Antony.'

'Andrew.'

'Agnes,' says Agnes. (Don't tell me she can *read*!)

Father Raimbaut, the sickly Cistercian, clears his throat beside her. He looks like something that's been buried for ten years, then dug up and left out in the rain.

'Adalbert of Prague,' he murmurs.

'No.' Frogface shakes her head. 'I was an English archbishop –'

'Augustine!' Input from Corba, the merchant's widow. Heavily pious. A bundle of nerves wrapped up in fine wool. 'Oh, no – Augustine came from Rome . . .'

'Ambrose?' (Joscelin.)

'No. I was Archbishop of Canterbury –'

'Aelfric! Aelfric!' (Corba's getting over-excited.) 'Is it Aelfric?'

'Aelfric wasn't a saint. I was Archbishop of Canterbury, and I was stoned to death in Greenwich by the Danes.'

Long pause. This one's a real brain-strangler. Raimbaut chews his thumbnail.

'Anselm?' he suggests. 'What happened to Saint Anselm?'

'I give up,' says Agnes.

'So do I.' (Joscelin.)

'It must be Anselm. He was Archbishop of Canterbury.'

'No. Give up?'

'It's – um – it's –'

'Yes, we give up,' says Agnes. 'Who is it?'

'It's Saint Alphege!'

A chorus of groans. Father Raimbaut looks disgusted. 'I knew it,' he says. 'It was on the tip of my tongue . . .'

'Your turn, Mistress Agnes.' Frogface, graciously. 'If you think you can . . .?'

'Right.' Agnes is the colour of minced beef, and shiny with sweat, but she looks a lot more cheerful than her donkey – whose knees are beginning to tremble under the combined weight of Agnes, Gerald and a hearty breakfast. 'This is really difficult. I learned it from a nun and it will destroy you. Which saint am I? My name begins with "U"–'

'Ursula!'

'No.'

'No?' Frogface can't believe her ears. 'But that's the only "U" there is!'

'I said it was difficult.'

'Urban?' (Raimbaut.) 'One of the popes?'

'No. I was a bishop –'

'Oh!' Frogface almost falls off her donkey. 'I know! I know! *Ulrich of Augsberg!*'

'No. I was Bishop of Samosata, and I was killed by a blow on the head from an Aryan heretic in Syria.'

A long, long silence. Brains are wracked. Faces fall.

No one has any suggestions.

'We give up,' says Joscelin.

'Yes, we give up.'

'I knew you would.' Agnes beams. 'It's Saint *Eusebius!*'

Saint who? (Didn't even know there was one.) People glance at each other, embarrassed by their own ignorance. Father Raimbaut frowns.

'Wait a minute.' He sounds puzzled. 'Saint Eusebius was a Roman pope. He died in Sicily.'

'Oh no, Father. The nun told me. He died in Syria.'

'Unless there were two of them . . . What's his feast day?'

'Um – now she told me that, too. Let me think . . .'

I wonder if anyone's going to point out the obvious?

Agnes furrows her brow over the problem, until she works out that the feast day was on June twenty-first. Aha! That explains it. Raimbaut's saint has *his* feast day on the seventeenth of August. Clearly they're two entirely different saints. But it's no good – I can't hold back any longer.

'Excuse me. Doesn't Eusebius begin with an "E"?'

Father Raimbaut slaps his forehead. Of course! It turns out that Agnes can't read, though she does know the sound of one or two letters. I didn't think this game was going to get very far.

'Pagan.'

Duty calls. He's a pace or two ahead, trying to maintain a professional silence. You can tell he's displeased by the way his nostrils twitch.

Time to kick a little speed into this idle nag.

'I have asked you to stay close to me, Pagan.' Solemnly. 'Please keep this in mind.'

'Yes, my lord.'

'And I would prefer it if you didn't talk to the pilgrims. We are *not* here to entertain them.'

(Come again?)

'But I didn't!'

'I heard you. Now I believe Brother Tibald talked about brigands in yesterday's chapter of squires. Is that correct?'

'Yes, my lord.'

'Did he talk about the Valley of Running?'

'No, my lord.' (At least I don't think he did.)

Saint George lifts an eyebrow. Something tells me I must have missed the bit about the Valley of Running.

'The Valley of Running lies between here and the Jordan,' he explains. 'It is a narrow and very dangerous gorge which brigands tend to favour when they ambush our escorts.'

'I think I've heard of it.'

'Good. So can you tell me what is the best method of defence on such a road?'

Damn, damn, damn. If I'd known we were going to be *tested*, I'd have paid more attention to Rockhead's talk. This is like Saint Joseph's all over again.

'Well?'

'Well, my lord . . . I think the best method of defence would probably be to run like hell.'

A long, long silence. Saint George seems to be choosing his words with care.

'Speed *is* essential.' (Unenthusiastically.) 'But it's more than a matter of speed, Pagan. When you're moving fast, it's the vanguard which becomes the archers' target, while those in the centre are exposed to the full force of the running attack. So it's important to put the shields up front, and the swords behind them. Do you understand?'

'Yes, my lord.'

'That's why I'll be putting you in front when we approach the Valley. You will *not* be required to stay near me. I shall be stationed behind, on the right flank. You are not to turn back on any account: you will form part of our arrowhead, and you must cut straight through. Do you understand?'

Oh, I understand, all right. Can't handle a sword, but good enough for target practice. Same old story.

'Yes, my lord. I understand.'

He falls silent. Not a single bead of sweat on his brow, though it's as hot as hell's kitchen. Not a breath of wind. Fans flap. Children whine. Horseflies drone like monks at prayer. If I was a brigand, I wouldn't be out boiling my brains in this sun. I'd have my feet up in some nice, cool cave, with a jug of lime juice and a damp cloth over my eyes.

'Pagan?'

(What *now*?)

'I heard you say something to those pilgrims . . .' Pause. 'Am I to understand that you can *read*?'

'Yes, my lord. I can read.'

'And write, too?'

'Yes, my lord.'

Another brief silence. That wide, blue stare: wide, blue and empty, like the desert sky.

'I suppose you were taught at the monastery, when you were a child?'

(Well I certainly didn't learn it in the guardroom.)

'Yes, my lord.'

He nods. Behind us, the pilgrims are growing restless. Agnes, especially. There's no mistaking those dulcet tones.

'Let's sing!' she squawks. 'I always like a good sing-along.'

'What about Psalm Forty-Six?' (Frogface.) 'What about "There is a river the streams whereof shall make glad the City of God"?'

'No, no.' Naturally Joscelin has to put his word in. (Poisonous little scorpion.) 'We should sing Psalm Fifty-Three. "Corrupt are they, and have done abominable iniquity." After all, we'll be passing the ruins of Gomorrah, soon.'

Gomorrah! Thrills! Excitement! A babble of questions! Where? Where is it? Can we see it? Can you show it to us?

Meanwhile Joscelin – the expert – takes it all in his stride. If anyone knows about Sodom and Gomorrah, it's the man who should have been born there.

'No, it's not far. It's down to the south,' he says. 'You can see the Pillar of Salt two parasangs from the Dead Sea.'

'The Pillar of Salt? You mean Lot's wife? The real Lot's wife?' Corba can't believe her ears. 'Where she was turned to salt for gazing at God's vengeance on the Cities of the Plain?'

'That's right.'

'And you can *see* her?'

'That's right.'

Awestruck silence – but not for long.

'What does she look like?'

The scorpion rolls his eyes skyward like a dying cow.

'She looks brave and tormented and beautiful,' he drivels – forgetting the fact that he's never been farther south than Hebron in his entire life. I have, though. I've also seen the Pillar of Salt. And if that was Lot's wife, she was a midget hunchback with one leg missing.

'Can we visit her?' Frogface inquires.

'Alas no.' Joscelin shakes his head. 'The Infidel lurks in that region during the warm months. But miraculously, although the sheep are always licking it, the pillar always grows back again. So you can take as much salt away as you like. And I happen to know a man who can sell you half a pound of Lot's wife, beautifully presented in a hand-crafted salt cellar made from the famous Tyrian green ware –'

Christ in a cream cheese sauce. Doesn't he ever give up? Saint George clears his throat, loudly. I suspect it's the closest he's ever come to shoving his fist down a pilgrim's throat and ripping his tonsils out.

'Sergeant Gildoin!'

'My lord?'

'We'll call a rest break, I think. Women to the north, men to the south.'

'Yes, my lord.'

'And make it fast.'

Which is easy enough for *him* to say. If you ask me, Saint George the Man of Marble doesn't even *have* a bladder. If you ask me, he doesn't perform any natural functions at all.

Some people seem to think you can't drown in the Jordan.

It's quite shallow now, of course – thick and sluggish between stretches of dry, brown mud – but it's still water. If God had meant us to inhale it, He would have given us gills. You can't tell that to the pilgrims, though. It's like reasoning with a herd of mad donkeys.

'God's pilgrims!' Saint George makes a futile attempt to stem the tide. 'Please dismount and proceed in an *orderly* fashion to the riverbank, taking care to remain within calling distance . . .'

Pointless, of course. Might as well ask an avalanche to please turn round and go home. The hairy fanatic is first off the mark: heads straight for the shallows and keeps running. Gildoin gives chase on horseback. Meanwhile Agnes has hit the water (whoosh! like a sheep in a well), followed by Corba

and Radulf and a gaggle of children. The force of the rearguard push throws some of these children completely off their feet. Mothers lurch in after them. Old men go under. A blind girl panics. Elbows connect violently with foreheads.

Last one in's a dirty Infidel!

No wonder the brigands didn't attack us in the Valley of Running. Why bother, when all they have to do is sit back and wait for us to commit suicide?

'Pagan! Over here!'

Saint George to the rescue. He's already thigh-deep in a boiling mass of water, mud and bodies, fishing out toddlers by the hair. Very calm, of course. Takes more than forty drowning pilgrims to panic the Man of Marble.

'Nun, Pagan!'

Nun, Pagan. Four steps to the right, flat on her face, too weak to haul herself out of the mud. Pulled down by the weight of her wet robes. Hard to get a firm hold – and the mud is like glue. One step (slurp). Two steps (slurp). Drag her up by the wimple. Half dead already. Gasping for breath and groping for support. Old and fat and hard to move.

'Oi! Hey! Can I have a bit of help here?'

Sergeant – what's his name? Gaspard? Gregory? – staggers over to lend a hand. Takes the feet while I take the shoulders. (Hups-a-daisy!) Six steps to dry land. Drop her like a sack of bricks. Then back to the battle. But what's left to do? The children are safe, restored to their mothers. Gildoin's rescued our hairy fanatic. The last old man's being hauled ashore. No casualties, by the look of it. Saint George is collecting the bottles and rags still afloat on the choppy water. A *very* smart move. Leave them to drift and we'll have

the whole lot in again, trying to rescue their precious possessions.

Quick glance around: no lurking brigands. No wolves. A guard's been mounted (when did he give the orders?) and Welf's rounding up stray donkeys. Someone's thumping an old woman's back. Father Raimbaut in shock. Frogface. Radulf . . .

Joscelin.

Hasn't lifted a finger. Still in the saddle, calm, cool, collected.

If only I'd moved faster, he could have been drowned by now.

'God's pilgrims!' Saint George dumps an armload of wet luggage onto the riverbank. He looks a little grim around the mouth. 'There is a belief held by some ignorant people that only Infidels drown in the Jordan, because these are the waters wherein stood the feet of the priests who bore the Ark of the Covenant. Unfortunately, such people are *seriously mistaken.*'

Gerald starts to cry, setting off a whole, dismal chorus. It's hard to believe that most of the Templars in this escort actually *volunteered* their services.

'Many Christians have drowned in the holy river you see here,' Saint George continues (raising his voice), 'so for your own safety I am not permitting anyone to enter the water any higher than their knees. Is that understood?'

Despondent murmurs. No one's going to argue, though. You don't feel too assertive when you're sitting in a puddle of mud.

'When the sun moves behind that tree we'll be leaving,' Saint George concludes. 'Kindly stay between the two

guards on horseback. And remember that each pilgrim is allowed no more than eight full bottles of holy water. Sergeant Maynard will be counting each load before we depart.

'Thank you – that is all.'

Pilgrims, pilgrims, pilgrims. You wonder what they expect to find here. You wonder if they're ever disappointed. Do they know about the Patriarch of Jerusalem? Do they know that this so-called man of God chases after every woman in sight? Do they know that every second blind man begging on the streets around here can see just as well as I do? That for every genuine saint's relic on sale, there are five hundred worthless bits of rag and bone selling for the same price?

Look at them, filling their bottles. Bathing their crippled limbs. So pathetic, really. Too dense to be afraid, even in the Valley of Running. Singing cheerful little psalms as we wind our way through that steep-sided gorge, where the earth is black and salty with the blood of dead pilgrims.

'Excuse me.'

A woman, heading my way. Skinny, squinting, face like a trip to the city dump. Frankish, by the sound of it. Slopping around in unsuitable footwear.

'Excuse me, Master Templar, it's about those bottles. The bottles of holy water we can take back with us . . .'

Deaf, perhaps? Or just a bit simple?

'You're allowed eight.' (How many more times?) 'Eight bottles each.'

'Yes, but – I have a sister, you see. She's ill. And I promised to bring some holy water back for her.'

'Well you can, can't you? Or don't you have a bottle?'

'Yes, I have many bottles. So does my husband. But I

already promised my aunt. And her son-in-law. And my mother and my husband's stepbrother and our parish priest, and my cousin, because he gave us money for the pilgrimage –'

'All right. So what's the trouble?' (Afraid of draining the river? It's not the Red Sea, you know.)

She sidles up like a hungry dog, all grinning teeth and pleading eyes.

'Can't we take just one extra bottle?' she whines. 'Just one?'

'No.'

'It's only small, look –'

'Sorry.'

The hackles rise.

'We come all this way across the ocean, and now you say we can't take a drop of holy water back to my suffering sister?'

'Listen. I don't give the orders, understand? It's nothing to do with me.'

'And what if my sister dies? If my sister dies, God will know who killed her!'

Christ in a cream cheese sauce. I don't have to listen to this.

'Lady, if your sister's so damned sick, why can't your husband's stepbrother do without?'

'When his poor wife's as barren as a beef bone? I *promised* him some *genuine* Jordan water –'

'Dame Helvis.'

Joscelin. Sneaking up from behind like a cutpurse. Angelic smile on his face. No mud on his clothes. Mischief on his mind.

'Dame Helvis, you can still have your genuine Jordan water.'

She turns. 'I can?' This has got to stop. Right now.

'*March*, maggot.'

'You see, I too am allowed my ration of eight bottles.' Joscelin ploughs on, ignoring me. 'So I can take some of the precious liquid back for you. And it will only cost you three dinars a bottle.'

'*Three dinars?* But I can get it here for *free!*'

'Only eight bottles, though. You heard what Master Pagan said. And you must realise there's a very great demand for Jordan water – especially now that the trip here is so perilous. Demand is outstripping supply. I can get five dinars for every bottle I bring back from this journey. So you see, I'm making a very generous offer.'

She looks him up and down, spits at his feet. No sale.

'Call yourselves Christians!' she hisses. 'You filthy hypocrite Turcopole soft-bellied traitors!' And she waddles away through the mud, puffing and blowing like an angry plough-horse.

Joscelin smiles at her retreating back.

'Stinking brainless slug-faced bitch,' he mutters. 'Of course you know what she wants it for, don't you? That holy water. She wants it to sell when she gets back home. She can recoup her outlay threefold, if she does. It's quite common.'

'Take a walk, maggot.'

'You surely don't believe that tale about the sister?'

'I said take a walk. *Now.*'

'Before I do, Pagan, there's something we ought to discuss. And I promise I'll make it worth your while.'

'There's nothing we have to discuss.'

He grabs my arm as I turn away. It's like having a leech crawl down the back of your neck.

'Get *off* me!'

'All right, all right. Don't upset yourself. I just want to make a proposition. A *paying* proposition.'

He leans so close that I can feel his hot breath on my face. Still gargling perfume, to judge from the stink. Still using scent in his hair oil. Sweet and sickly, like the smell of gangrene. So strong I can hardly draw breath.

'Didn't I tell you to stay downwind?'

'Listen, Pagan. You need cash, or you wouldn't be playing mother to a lot of half-wits. Now I can help, if you'd just lend me an ear.'

'An *ear*? What would you do with an ear, sell it off as a relic?'

'Pagan –'

'I've had your kind of "help" before, you bloodsucker. And I don't want any more of it.'

'All you have to do is put in a good word for me, Pagan. That's all.' He's like a wasp, hovering and buzzing. 'You're on pilgrimage escort, aren't you? Well I need pilgrims. It's the perfect relationship. You recommend me to your pilgrims as a guide, and I'll give you a cut of their fee. Say, twenty per cent. You'll have all the money you need in a month. *Under* a month. We could make a *fortune*. You know how everyone trusts a Templar . . .'

Buzz, buzz, buzz. I can hardly hear him through the hum of the flies. It's still stinking hot, and you can smell the river. The sweat's stinging my sunburned neck. My boots are full of mud. I'm in the dead heart of brigand country, shackled to a herd of blind cripples.

What the hell am I doing here?

'...could even make it official, perhaps. Get me appointed. Official Escort Guide. Ask your knight what their position is...'

My knight is mounting guard. Thought I'd lost him, for a moment, but he's up on the rise behind us, strategically stationed. Sitting up there on his white horse like a statue at the Gates of Paradise, all white and gleaming gold. Scanning the horizon with his blue hawk's eyes. Any moment now he's going to see who I'm with.

I must be mad, listening to this rubbish.

'...make it thirty per cent, if you like. Thirty per cent for practically nothing. What have you got to lose? Think about it, Pagan...'

'I've thought about it, bog-breath. And do you know what I think?' Slowly. Quietly. 'I wouldn't ask for your help if I was drowning in a vat of manure. Understand? So get your festering carcass out of my way, or I'll slice it up and feed it to the vultures.'

Nice to have a good, solid piece of metal at your hip, in these situations. Nobody argues with a Solingen sword. I don't even have to unsheathe it and he moves aside, swallowing the poison on his adder's tongue.

Time to go and pull a bit of weight. Round up a few stray pilgrims. After all, that's what I'm here for.

Chapter 3

Squeak, squeak, squeak. Chink of harness. Smell of hot leather. One stupid fly that's on a fast horse to hell, if it so much as sets *foot* on my bottom lip again. Slumping in the saddle with a pain in my back, because I haven't ridden this kind of distance in two years, minimum.

Saint George up ahead, sitting as straight as an arrow.

You've got to admit he rides well. Probably *born* with a horse between his legs. Fully armed. Hard to imagine what kind of parents could have produced such a paragon. Lord Valiant and Lady Virtue. Most courteously married in the Castle of Chivalry. Baby Roland, tutored by twelve wise men (Patience, Courage, Faith, Hope, Charity, Justice, Wisdom, Etiquette, Cleanliness, Thrift, Good Taste and Perfect Table Manners), piously raised as a living dedication to God. Weaned on the sacred host and holy water.

His only playmate, a statue of Saint Sebastian.

Saint Sebastian, the Roman soldier. Killed by arrows. Saint George's wound is a fearsome thing – though he seems to sit quite easily in the saddle. A terrible scar, red and brown, still leaking onto a linen pad under his clothes. Across the right flank and into the stomach. Probably would have killed anyone else.

The hand of God, I wonder?

'*Pagan.*'

Whoops! 'Yes, my lord.'

'What are you doing? Concentrate, Pagan, we're almost at the Valley.'

So we are. Should have felt the tension. Saint George has fallen back to keep pace with me.

'A trick for the future, Pagan. If you're on a long ride and you feel your mind wandering, start counting the bends in the road. Or the trees you pass – if there aren't too many. Do you understand?'

'Yes, my lord.'

'It's wise to keep alert.' He glances over his shoulder. 'I should tell you,' he adds (lowering his voice), 'that if the brigands attack, they attack on the return journey. After they've judged our strength, and when the pilgrims are tired and weighed down with holy water.'

Terrific.

'We'll take our positions now. *Gildoin!*' A nod. (Gildoin pulls back a little, signals to the rearguard.) 'I want you in front with the shields again, Pagan, only this time remember to keep your shield right *up*, please. I don't want to see any face exposed. They'll be shooting from above, remember.'

He reins in, slowing, so he can fall back and join the middle escort behind us.

'My lord –'

'What?'

What? Good question. I don't know.

'Nothing.'

He waits for a moment.

'Is your shield too heavy?'

'No, no. It's all right.'

'You mustn't be disturbed by the noise these brigands make. It may sound like souls in torment, but it's only hot air. It means nothing.'

'My lord, I've heard Patriarch Heraclius singing hymns. Hell itself can't hold anything as horrible as the sound of his high notes.'

Brief pause. Then – could it be? Yes. No. Yes. I'm seeing things. A *miracle*.

Saint George is actually smiling.

O clap your hands all ye people and shout unto God with the voice of triumph. A proud moment in history, my friends. Lord Roland Roucy de Bram has delivered a small but healthy smile. No signs of stress or cracking in the facial area. Teeth remain in place. No nasty surprises. A brave and entertaining effort.

Gone now, but not forgotten.

'You are quite shameless, Pagan.' Seriously, with his mouth under control. Can't fool me, though. Now I *know* there's someone hiding inside that statue. Someone who's heard Heraclius sing. 'You should have more respect. Now go and take up your position, please. And keep your eyes open.'

You mean I can't keep them *shut*? But how else am I going to get through this business? Welf and Bonetus are up front, side by side, big and square but not big enough to hide behind. Welf in particular: built like a road fort, wrists as thick as your average pilgrim, skin the colour of a smoked eel. Practically bald under his helmet and missing two fingers and half an ear. Rather slow on the uptake, but a man to inspire confidence.

And Bonetus. Smaller, slimmer, quicker, fiercer. A temperament hotter than most Templar sergeants – or so they tell me. Nicknamed 'the Mace' because of the mace hanging from his saddle: vicious but lightweight, with a well-worn leather grip. Swinging back and forth, back and forth. Scrubbed clean of blood, hair, flesh, clothing.

Behind him, Sergeant Maynard. A living, walking apocalypse. Teeth like tombstones under his bloodshot glare. A ravaged crater of a face, dark, frozen, twisted. Extremely tall. Hardly human. They talk about Maynard in quiet corners, because his wife and two children were struck down with leprosy. He has fits himself, sometimes, but not violent ones. Only Saint George can look him in the eye for long.

They say he fights like a panther in a sheep-pen.

Welf, Bonetus, Maynard. With a line-up like this, what do they need *me* for? I'm only going to get in the way. I'm only going to damage their invincible image, like a lame puppy trailing after a victory procession. You can see Bonetus is thinking the same thing. You can tell by the way he orders me to fall in behind him.

Saint George gives the signal, and we raise our shields.

The Valley, deep in shadow. An afternoon chill falls onto the pilgrims, subduing them, shutting their mouths at long last. The echo of horseshoes clinking on loose rocks. The whimper of a weary child, way back in the column. Someone sneezes. A glance at Saint George: he's guarding the left flank, stone-faced. Doesn't look too worried. (But then he never does.) Hand on his sword hilt. Eyes on the move. Sees me looking and jerks his head. Turn around, Pagan. You're supposed to be watching the road.

But there's nothing to report – nothing of interest. If they're going to attack, why not get it over with? Nothing stirs behind the brush and boulders. A pilgrim starts praying. 'God is our refuge and our strength, a very present help in trouble. Therefore we will not fear . . .' Speak for yourself, stupid.

A bend in the road. A blind corner. Could this be it? There's a shifting of postures, a rustle of fabric, as muscles tighten all over the escort.

Still nothing.

If I were a brigand, I wouldn't take on a party like this. I'd rather raid villages. No Templars in villages. Hardly any men either, nowadays. You can do what you like in a place like that. Burn, rape, pillage. God knows it's been done before. I suppose I wouldn't *be* here, if it hadn't.

Sudden thought. What if I were attacked, here and now, by my very own father? What if dear old Dad came screaming down that dusty slope, swinging an axe-head? What a laugh that would be. Not that I've ever laid eyes on the pus-bag. But maybe I'd know all the same. Maybe you can *tell*, somehow. Blood will out. Blood to blood. Maybe I'd recognise myself in his cheekbones.

Childhood dream: to grow up, get strong, and hang my father's guts out to dry. Who knows? Perhaps that dream is about to come true. Perhaps he's just around the corner, slavering into his bloodstained beard. Not *quite* as strong as he used to be . . .

'Look there!'

Action stations!

No. False alarm. One of the pilgrims has spotted a scattering of bones by the roadside. Could be human, could be animal. No rags or horns to give you any clue. Welf and Bonetus exchange glances.

'Keep moving.' Saint George raises his voice as the procession slows. '*Move along, please.*'

'Should we not collect them? Just in case?' Father Raimbaut addresses Saint George, who shakes his head silently. The bones are grey and splintered, very old. Dust to dust. Leaving them behind, rounding the last corner. The road widens. Ahead – the gateway. Dramatic pillars of rock, crowned with sunlight. Beyond them, an easy, gradual, spreading, rolling fall to level ground.

Somebody wants to empty his bladder. Permission withheld. No stopping until we've cleared the Valley. Not long now, though. Nearly there. The pace quickens . . .

O Blessed be the Lord my strength, which teacheth my hands to war and my fingers to fight; my goodness and my fortress, my high tower and my deliverer, my shield and he in whom I trust.

It looks like we've made it.

'So what do *you* have left? Or are you finished?'

'No, we're not finished. We've still got Mount Sion, and Our Lady of Josophat, and the Pool of Bethesda. And the shrine of the Ascension.'

'Oh, haven't you seen the shrine yet? Oh, you must. They've got the autograph text of the Lord's prayer.'

'And what about the Abbey of Latina? Are you seeing that too?'

'Well ... we don't really know if we're going to have the time ...'

'Anyway, there's not much to see inside, is there?'

'There certainly is! When the Blessed Virgin fainted at the crucifixion she was carried to a cave under the abbey, and when she woke up she tore out a handful of hair, and they've got it there in a golden casket.'

'Really? You think it's worth seeing?'

'Oh, absolutely.'

'Well maybe we'll skip the Church of Saint Peter's Chains, and do the Abbey of Latina instead.'

'Saint Peter's Chains! Don't bother with Saint Peter's Chains, it's in a shocking condition. A real dump. You can't even see the relics, it's so dark.'

Et cetera, et cetera. Pilgrim talk. Most of them are on a pretty tight schedule, with lots to do in just a couple of days. The Jordan trip has left them with very little time to kiss the Holy Sepulchre, or cast their wooden crosses onto Calvary, or pile up rocks in the Valley of Hinnom (where they hope to sit enthroned on the Day of Judgement). Some have overspent on relics and souvenirs, and are down to their last dinars. For them, Gaspard has a list of certified charities like Saint John's Hospital, or the Hospice of the Agony in the Garden.

Only for genuine cases, though. Woe betide anyone who's hiding money in their shoes or hats or underwear.

'Thank you, Brother. Thank you kindly.'

'And the Hospital's just down there, you say?'

'Down there, first left, second right, then take the first stairs.'

'Thank you, Brother.'

'Thank you, Brother.'

Back inside the walls again. Back to the Cattle Market, knee-deep in dung. Most of the pens are empty once more, but the sheep have left some strong-smelling traces behind them. It's been a busy day at the sale yards. You can tell by the piles of gnawed fruit stones and sugar cane; the choppy mess of footprints in the mud around the water troughs; the cluster of shepherds drinking away their profits under an awning. There's an argument going on between the Collector of Tolls and someone who doesn't want to pay his trading taxes. Someone in a silk burnous. Sackcloth is better if you want to win an argument like *that*, my friend. Sackcloth, sores and tearstains.

'Goodbye, Master Templar.'

Trapped! A round red face, a man-eating smile, a slobbering infant. Agnes the Dreaded. Bearing Gerald the Unclean like some kind of gift in her arms.

No, dear, I'm not kissing *anything* covered with strands of goo. I joined the Templars to fight Infidels, not to face the ultimate horror.

'Goodbye, Mistress Agnes.' (Shouldn't have dismounted. Should have stayed on my horse, beyond the reach of sticky children.) 'I hope your trip was beneficial.'

'Oh yes, I think so. I think it was.' She doesn't sound

too sure. 'Of course Radulf's backache hasn't cleared up yet, but we didn't really *pray* for that. Perhaps we should have. But we haven't seen all the sacred sites, so there's still time, I suppose. Before we leave . . .'

'That's good.' God preserve us. Is she going to drivel on all day? Quick glance around. Saint George is out of earshot, wrestling with a minor crisis. Pilgrims baying for blood, by the look of it. Could someone be missing? Or has the Jordan failed to deliver enough in the way of miracles?

Keep clear of *that* little dust-up.

'. . . it was like dysentery, only not so watery – more mushy, I suppose. Poor Gerald. So I gave him some holy water mixed with gruel . . .'

Christ in a cream cheese sauce!

'Excuse me, Mistress Agnes, but I have to – urn – to –' To what? To get the hell out of here, that's what. Sudden glimpse of a hand, beckoning. Joscelin's hand. What's *he* doing, still hanging round the markets? I thought he'd scuttled back to his dunghill long ago. 'I have to talk to someone. It's very important. I'm sorry. Goodbye and good luck.'

Anything to escape. At least Joscelin doesn't talk about his bowel movements. He's lurking at the mouth of that dank, unwholesome alley which leads to St Mary of the Germans: the alley which smells of camels and latrines. Propping up somebody's warehouse wall. Lazily flapping the flies away with a whisk made of horsehair and sandalwood. Flick, flick, flick.

'Well? What is it?'

'Lower your voice, Pagan.'

'I'll count to five. One – two –'

'Listen to me.' Softly. Grabbing my arm, falling back into the shadows. 'I have some information . . .'

'Get off.'

'It's confidential. People would pay big money for this. People like the Templars. We could split the reward.'

'What do you mean? What reward?'

He looks uneasy. His eyes jump like fleas from body to body as he scans the marketplace.

'Just come back here, will you? I don't want anyone to see us together.'

(You and me both, bog-brain.)

'All right. But this had better be good . . .'

It's like entering someone's intestines. Narrow, slimy, smelling of dung. A cloud of flies settling like a cloak over your head and shoulders. Bones. Rats. Sludge from the nearby tannery. A glorified gutter, as black as the Queen of Sheba's armpit.

A murderer's alley.

Stop. Wait. Think. Up ahead, Joscelin disappears around a corner.

I don't like the look of this.

To hell with it. Turn around. Jerked back. Grip on the collar: slip in the scum. Knees hit the paving. Sword! Sword!

'Oh no you don't.'

Crack. Down. Can't breathe. Weight on the head. Choking . . . 'Oof!' Jesus! Oh Jesus. They've broken my ribs.

'Lost something, Kidrouk?'

Voice of the monster. God preserve us.

'I'm *talking* to you.'

Weight's lifted. Turn my head . . . Bervold. And Hamo,

who's swinging my sword. Bervold's got a plank of wood –
with nails in it. God preserve us. Hamo half drunk,
red-eyed, grinning.

'Maybe we can trade.' (Bervold.) 'Your weapon for my
money. *Now.*'

Trying to think.

'*Now,* you scum-bucket!'

Wood. Duck. *Slam!* Elbow. Agony. Groaning.
Writhing.

Taste of rot on my teeth. Rot from the pavement.

'The money.' Bervold leans over, grabs a handful of
hair. '*Where's the money?*'

'*I'll* get it . . . I'll get it . . .'

'No – *I'll* get it. Just tell me where it is.'

'I mean – I mean – when I get paid . . .'

Pause.

'When you get *paid*?' Slowly. 'When you get paid? Hear
that, Hamo? When he gets paid.'

'Ha ha.'

'I'm afraid that's not good enough, Kidrouk. I'm afraid
we can't wait that long.'

Up – up – dragged by the hair. Jerking. Pulling. Like
red-hot pins in your scalp.

Kick out. No contact. Hamo laughs.

'You want a *fight*, butterfly?'

God. They're going to kill me. Deliver me, O Lord,
from the evil man. Preserve me from the violent –

'Oow!'

Hit the wall. Slide down . . . Where? In the belly. Boot
in the belly. Coughing. Wood again. *Crack!* Stars. Paralysed.
Hauled up. Fist. Grin.

'Say your prayers, pig-swill.'

Shut my eyes and wait. And wait. Nothing. Still nothing. Sneak a look through my lashes.

Bervold's face, frozen. Blank. A shiny blade just grazing his left cheekbone.

I know that blade. I'd know it anywhere. I've cleaned it myself with rags and lard and bunches of chain.

'All right.' A soft, familiar voice. 'Let him go. *Gently*.'

Saint George saves the day. Gleaming white, rock-faced, hard as a diamond. Calm. Steady. The avenging angel.

Eat dirt, Bervold.

'Let him go, or lose an ear.'

'*Look out!*'

Flash of steel – Roland whirls – Hamo lunges – Roland parries. *Clang*. The force of the Templar blade sends my sword spinning from Hamo's clumsy grip. Now Bervold moves. Launches himself at Roland's back and *thud!* Connects with an elbow.

Reels away, gasping. Bent like a cripple. Roland turns, so fast – can't see – one knee jerks up and straight to the jaw. Crunch. Bone on bone. Bervold drops as Hamo charges, waving his wood. But Roland's swung round to meet him. Sword up. Aimed at the belly.

Hamo stops.

'Well?' says Roland.

Behind him Bervold is crawling away, struggling to his feet, escaping like a wounded animal. Hamo roars. He hurls his wood and runs for his life, grabbing Bervold, dragging him, roaring, spitting, frenzied with fear.

Roland's dodged the flying wood. He doesn't give chase. He takes a few steps, slows, stops. Breathing heavily,

but with his mouth shut. Watching the two men retreat.

You could lay a bet on what he's thinking. (No point wasting energy on *that* scum.) His eyes drop to his sword: he examines it, quickly but carefully. Wipes the blade on the skirts of his tunic. Restores the weapon to its sheath.

And swings round, stony-faced. Like God at the Last Judgement.

Now it's my turn.

'Does it hurt there?'

'Ouch!'

'What about here?'

'Ow!'

'And if I move this? Does that hurt?'

'*Yeow!*'

God preserve us! It's like being punched up all over again. I thought infirmaries were supposed to make people better, not torture them to death.

'All right.' A greasy ear on my ribs. 'Breathe in. Deeper. Now breathe out. And in. Keep breathing. Keep breathing . . .'

Keep breathing. As if I was going to *stop* breathing! I'd be in trouble if I did, Brother Gavin, let me tell you. Or haven't you worked that out yet?

'Hmmm.' He straightens, frowning. 'And does it hurt when you breathe?'

'Yes.'

'In or out?'

'Both.'

'There *could* be a cracked rib. It's hard to tell. But there's nothing broken. Nothing ruptured either, or you'd be dead by now.'

Terrific.

'Just a few bruises. Not severe. If they swell at all I can apply a few leeches, but at the moment I'd recommend a poultice. Just the usual. Hyssop and wormwood, wax and vinegar, a little comfrey – maybe a touch of marjoram.'

Christ in a cream cheese sauce.

'To *drink*?'

'Don't be a fool, boy. It's a fomentation. A dressing.' (To Roland.) 'I'll strap a couple on now, and change them tomorrow morning. If you can send him along then, my lord?'

He doesn't wait for a reply, moving to the shelves in the corner. They're loaded with pottery jars, all labelled: lovage, elder, iris, anise, dittany, hellebore, fennel, rue, dill, hemlock, belladonna, rosemary . . . no wonder the whole room stinks like a dog's breath. And the floor's covered in strewing herbs, scattered among the rushes. Steam and smoke, mortars and pestles, wet rags and goose grease. Hot as hell because the fire's always burning.

Brother Gavin's domain.

He looks like something God put together at the end of the Seventh Day, with leftover scrapings. Shorter than I am. Arms of a giant, legs of a dwarf, huge, hairy ears and a dainty maiden's nose. The eyebrows and neck seem to be missing. He's quick on his feet, though. From shelf to table, table to fireplace. Whizz, whizz, whizz. A sprig of hyssop, a half-cup of vinegar, crushed wormwood, a block of wax, mash together over a slow heat. Chattering cheerfully.

'Was there trouble today on the escort, my lord?'

'Trouble? No.'

'Really? Training then, I suppose.'

Lord Roland frowns, puzzled.

'Training?'

'The bruises...'

'Oh.'

Will he or won't he? A blank, blue stare. So far he's said nothing. No questions, no lectures, no nothing. But if he's going to throw me out, why bandage me up first? He must *know* I'm a dead man the moment I set foot outside these headquarters.

'Yes,' he says at last. 'Yes, it was a training exercise. Defensive manoeuvres. He's not very good at them.'

'That's easy enough to see, my lord. I hope it's taught him a lesson...'

Chatter, chatter. Empty words. Gavin dips bandages into his ointment. Folds them over my belly and shoulder. Straps them on using more torn linen.

Lord Roland watches with folded arms. Not a flicker of feeling. Talk, you louse. Why don't you talk? Wouldn't let *me* talk. Are we going to forget this ever happened? Save it, you said. Save it for when?

I can't think of a good lie to tell him. Passing thieves? He won't believe that. Jealous husband? That's even worse. I'm so tired, I just can't think.

'Right.' Gavin steps back, wiping his hands on his tunic. 'That about does it. I'll give you a draught to help you sleep, and you should take an extra blanket to bed with you. I have one here, if you like...'

'That won't be necessary.' Lord Roland wakens from

his trance. 'Thank you, Brother. Your skill has been invaluable, as always.'

A compliment for Gavin: a curt nod for me. (Put your clothes on, scum-bucket.) Hobbling after him like a drunken leper, through the door, past the kitchens, across the courtyard. Golden lights in the dusk. A gentle murmur from the Draper's office. Quiet. Cosy. Safe.

Deliver me from mine enemies, O my God; defend me from them that rise up against me. Deliver me from the workers of iniquity, and save me from bloody men. For lo, they lie in wait for my soul; the mighty are gathered against me.

The door to his chamber – his and mine. My palliasse near the tiny window. My blanket, my cup, my spoon. Mine but not mine. I suppose they'll go to someone else when I leave.

'Sit down, Pagan.'

Easier said than done, of course. He lights an oil lamp as I lower my throbbing collection of bruises onto the bed (delicately, like a mother delousing her only child). And turns to face me.

'All right.' Folding his arms. 'I want the truth, Pagan. The whole story. From the beginning.'

The whole story, from the beginning. In the beginning there was the Word, and the Word was God. Once upon a time there was a boy called Pagan . . . How can I tell you the whole story, my lord? You wouldn't understand it. You're such a good man, you don't know what it's like to be bad.

'My lord, I owe some money.'

'What money?'

'Well – originally it was a gambling debt. But I paid *that* off with protection money. It's a bit hard to explain . . . Have you ever heard of the Silver Ring?'

'No.'

'I don't know much about them myself, but basically they're a bunch of villains who manage the trade in stolen goods on the fringes of the Latin Exchange. A lot of the pawnbrokers are involved. It's all very shady, as you can imagine.' (Or maybe you can't.) 'Anyway, they've always got people hanging around the cock fights and dice games, offering loans to the desperate. Like me. That's where I got involved with them. Thought I was on a winner. But I wasn't, of course, and I had to cough up the money or lose a couple of limbs. They're very dangerous people – if you know what I mean.'

'Go on.'

'Well, at that stage I was with the garrison. The city garrison. I used to patrol the Jewry quarter. Do you know the Street of the Flowers? You might think you do, but you don't really. It's the filthiest place – you wouldn't believe what goes on there. And it's allowed to go on because the Viscount of Jerusalem gets his cut of the profits. The Viscount and the Master-Sergeant. As long as *they* get paid, the filthier businesses can go about their . . . well, their business.'

Spare him the sordid details. It's a bit much already, by the look of things. Stunned gaze, knitted brows. Lord Roland is having trouble trying to grasp these unfamiliar concepts.

'Are you – have you proof of this?'

'My lord, we used to collect the Viscount's money ourselves. When we were on night patrol. That's how I

paid off the Silver Ring. I took the money I'd collected from one of these businesses, and then I pretended it hadn't paid up. They found out in the end, of course, but I managed to escape just in time. To these headquarters. They're the only safe place in the city, for me. Because no outsider can get in, and I never go out alone.'

So there it is. The unvarnished truth. You wanted it, you've got it – for all the good it does. Now what are you going to *do* with it, my lord? That's the big question.

'The men who attacked you . . . they were the *Viscount's* men?'

'My lord, they're from the garrison night watch. Just like me. They must have had their orders.'

'And what about that guide? The one who lured you into the ambush.'

So you were watching all the time, then? I'd never have known it.

'You mean Joscelin?' Good question. 'Joscelin's not on the night watch, my lord. I don't know *how* he got involved. Must have struck a deal with the Master-Sergeant, just in case I was on the Jordan escort. He might be paying protection money himself. I know he's in business somewhere around the Latin quarter.'

Roland shakes his head, walks to the window. Standing there with his hands on his hips. Straight. Solemn. Still in full armour. Oh well. At least if he *does* throw me out, I'll never have to clean that thrice-damned chain mail ever again.

He turns.

'Do you know, Pagan, that I can neither read nor write?'

(Beg your pardon?)

'My father cannot read, either. Nor my brothers. We were trained to fight, you see. And our priest was old and simple. He had forgotten most of his learning. We used to go to Abbot Cyprien when we needed help. A very wise, very learned man. A man most worthy of respect.'

He throws me one of those long, blue looks. One of those serious looks aimed straight at the heart.

'Do you understand what a wonderful gift you have been granted, Pagan? Do you understand how God has *blessed* you, with this gift of learning?'

Who, me? The butt of the backstreets? You're thinking of someone else, surely.

'My lord, I'd rather have been blessed with a strong right arm. Or fists like lead melons. Or even sharp fingernails would do. Something a bit *useful*.'

A reasonable request, I would have thought. Especially for someone in *my* condition. But he sighs, slowly, as if I'd just told him that tapeworms are human too.

'I don't know what I'm going to do with you, Pagan.' (Sounds familiar.) 'You're clumsy, you're untrained, you have no – no calling, no discipline, no discretion and no sense of responsibility. You have fallen among wicked men, and delighted in wicked deeds. I know you're young, but – Pagan, surely with your gift of learning, and your quickness of mind – you must have *seen* what you were doing. You must have chosen your own path. Only fools lose their way among sinners, Pagan, and you're no fool.'

God preserve us. This is worse than the beating. Why not give me the boot and have done with it? I can't stand this kind of thing.

He plants himself right in front of my nose, forcing my chin up.

'Look at me, Pagan.' (As if I had a choice!) 'God gave you learning for a reason. And He brought you to *me* for a reason. And I know He didn't turn you from the path to hell just so that I could throw you back into the maw of the Seven-Headed Beast. Do you understand what I'm saying? Pagan? Do you understand?'

'You're – you're going to let me stay? In the Order?'

'Yes. Because I am His servant in all things. And buzz, buzz, buzz, zzzz . . .'

Can't hear what he's saying. Head feels funny – like an inflated wineskin. Ears hum. Eyes swim. Sick with relief.

Literally.

'Excuse me, my lord.' Gasping. 'I think – I think I'm going to throw up . . .'

Nice move, Pagan. Show your undying gratitude by vomiting all over the poor man's bed-chamber floor.

Oh well – never mind. We all know who'll be cleaning it up afterwards. And it won't be Lord Roland Roucy de Bram.

Part Two
July, 1187

The kingdom of Jerusalem waits for news, as its King leads a great army into Galilee to fight the invader Saladin.

Part Two
July 1187

The kingdom of Jerusalem waits for
news as its king leads a great army
into battle to fight the army of Saladin.

Chapter 4

And on the eighth day the Lord God formed a man from a dungheap, and breathed into his nostrils the breath of life, and the dungheap became a living soul called Odo – who to this day retains all the nobility, wisdom and grace of the dungheap which fathered him.

Here he comes now: the walking dungheap. Exuding a smell of rotten vegetables. The charm of a dead cow, the wit of a swamp. Beside him, Arnulf. Arnulf the parsnip. Long, pale and stringy, with slimy black eyes like over-ripe olives dipped in oil. Slouching along in an outsize tunic, the skirts flapping limply around his calves. Kicking up the dust with his sandals.

What a splendid pair. What an inspiration. With these men on our side, who needs God?

'Hey!' The thick, clotted voice of the Dungheap. (He's seen me at last.) 'We've been looking for you! We've been looking all over! Where the hell have you been?'

It's no use replying. He probably wouldn't understand if I did. Arnulf's the one with the bigger brain, even though his head's a lot smaller. The Dungheap has a head like a side of beef with ears.

'What's up, Arnulf? Odo? Have you lost something? Your wits, maybe?'

'Ha ha. Very funny.' Arnulf shuffles over and sits down beside me on the bench. It's a small bench, stone, made for three normal people. But there's not enough room for the Dungheap's vast backside. He stands there, blocking the view.

'So what are *you* doing, pretty maid?' (Arnulf airs his stunted sense of humour.) 'Sewing your trousseau? Eh? Sewing your bridal gown?'

'That's right, Arn. I'm getting married tomorrow. Sergeant Tibald has asked me to be his wife.'

A soggy explosion of sniggers from Arnulf. The Dungheap just gawks. Wouldn't know a joke if it crawled up his nose and died there. Arnulf drags the robe from my lap. It's Lord Roland's indoor winter robe, long and plain, white wool with sleeves to the wrist. Pulled it out of the linen chest, this morning; checked it for moth holes; discovered that the hem had come down. So now I have to sew it up again.

Took me practically half a day just to thread the needle.

'Well now, isn't this a vision of loveliness?' Arnulf croons. 'Won't you look a picture in this?'

'Give it here, Arn.'

'Won't he look a picture, Odo?'

'Arn, that's Lord Roland's. Give it here.'

Someone emerges from the latrines. Sergeant Welf. He peers across the courtyard, sizing us up. Will he or won't he? Rockhead would. If it was Rockhead, we'd be licking the gutters clean by now. (The hand of the diligent shall bear rule, but the slothful shall be under tribute: Proverbs chapter twelve.) Welf, however, isn't one of nature's tyrants – though as a volunteer Templar he ranks above us all. He sniffs, in a neutral sort of way, and wipes his nose with the back of his hand. Then he moves off towards the stables.

All clear.

'Listen, you two. Don't you have something to keep yourselves occupied? Something dirty, perhaps? Or dangerous?' Even as I speak Arnulf spits, athletically. (You've got to admire the distance he covers.) 'Why don't you go and challenge the cook to a spit-off, Arn? First to hit the soup from twenty paces.'

Arnulf snorts.

'We *have* got something to do,' he says. 'But we need your help. We need three people.'

'If it's another roach race, you can count me out. They're not worth the effort.'

'Nah.' He lowers his voice, leaning closer. The pores on his face are cavernous. 'It's not a roach race. It's not rats, either. We just want to piss in Sergeant Tibald's helmet.'

Odo erupts. Giggling into his beard with a noise like sewage running down a drain. Best to pretend he's not there.

'The helmet's in his office, I suppose?' (Stalling.)

'The helmet's in his office, and *he's* in a chapter with the Under-marshal. We've checked.'

'All right. But what do you need three people for? His head isn't that big, is it? You wouldn't need three bladders full.'

'Ha ha. Very funny.'

'We've got to guard the approaches.' A kind word of explanation from the Dungheap. (Really, you know, he's as thick as sour milk.) 'There are two ways of reaching his room.'

'Oh, are there? Well thanks, Odo. Thanks for telling me.'

Arnulf rises.

'You coming, or not?' he says. 'We have to move fast.'

It's tempting. Very tempting. In fact you could almost say it was divine retribution.

'All right, I'll come. And I'll stand guard. But I'm not doing the business.'

Arnulf sneers – one of the ugliest sights in Christendom. His teeth look exactly like dead flies.

'What's the matter?' he says. 'You scared?'

'No, I'm not scared.' (You pin-headed louse.) 'But I can't piss while other people are listening, all right? Now let's go.'

Rockhead's office isn't far from Lord Roland's room. You cross the old cloister heading west, and it's in the new wing with the peaked roof, just next to the armoury. No one about, of course. Garrison numbers are depleted in any case, and at this time of the afternoon nearly everyone's down in the stables, worshipping their horses. Arnulf volunteers to guard the eastern approach.

'Pagan can watch the stairs,' he hisses, 'and Odo can do the job. If someone comes, just whistle. And when you're finished, Odo, you must collect me, and then we'll backtrack past Pagan and leave by the stairs. Got that?'

'Ummm . . . no.'

Once more for the Dungheap. No use hanging about. It's twenty-five paces to the top of the stairs. Past Rockhead's closed door, past the entrance to the armoury. All clear at this end. Someone's spilled lamp oil on the second step down – just where you're certain to slip on it. Strange that someone hasn't slipped already.

Perhaps I ought to clean it up . . .

'Hey! Hey Arnulf!'

The Dungheap. (Stupid fool. What's he shouting for?)

'Hey Arnulf, I can't get in!'

Well that's it, then. Pity. Wouldn't have expected a lock on the door. I mean, what's in there to guard? Except account books.

'Don't force it!' Arnulf's voice, echoing down the passage. Better see what's going on. Past the armoury (again), round the corner (again) . . . and there he is. Trying to stop Odo from breaking the door down. 'You can't open it, Odo, it's *locked*,' he says. 'There's a *lock* on it.'

'Then how do we get in?'

Good question. First good question the Dungheap's ever asked, I suspect. Time to make tracks.

'Come on, you two. Let's go.'

'Wait.' Arnulf's thinking. You can tell by the way his veins throb. 'What about the window?'

'The *window*?' (That arrow-slit?) 'Arnulf, it's about *two fingers wide*. You can't expect anyone to crawl through *that*.'

'No, but – well, if you could just aim properly . . .'

Christ in a cream cheese sauce.

'You *must* be *joking*.'

'Pagan?'

Dead shock.

It's Lord Roland.

'What are you doing?'

Standing there in his long white robe. What am I doing? Glance at Arnulf. No help there. All the blood's drained from his head to his ankles.

Come on, Pagan, think.

'We – we were looking for Sergeant Tibald, my lord.'

'Well he's not here. He's with Sergeant Pons. What did you want him for?'

'Oh – it was just a question. About our pay.'

'I see.' His blue eyes drop to the bundle in my arms. 'Have you finished with that tunic?'

'Uh – no, my lord.'

'Then I suggest you keep your question for later. When you've completed your task.' A long, hard stare for the Dungheap, who goggles back like a sun-struck mule. Arnulf examines his toenails. 'I'm sure these men have their own jobs to do. Is that not so, sergeant?'

It's a tough one. Will the Dungheap's brain collapse under the pressure? But Arnulf takes his arm to lead him away, and Lord Roland waits in silence until they're out of sight.

He looks a little pinched around the nostrils – as if he's just smelt something unpleasant.

'I hope you're not spending too much time with those men,' he murmurs. 'I doubt you'll benefit from their acquaintance.'

'Oh really? Do you know them, my lord?'

'Of course not.' (Perish the thought.) 'But I'm familiar with their . . . they have a reputation. A bad one. They are of dubious character, and are therefore unsuitable companions.'

Are they indeed?

'If they're dubious characters, my lord, what are they doing in the Order?'

Whoops! Just a little too artless. He raises an eyebrow. 'I hope you're not questioning our *judgement*, Pagan?'

'No, my lord.'

'Take my advice. Do not associate with such people. They have nothing to offer a person of your intelligence.'

Well I'm glad *you* think so. Trailing after him as he moves down the corridor. Fighting the urge to pull a face at his back.

'I know I haven't given enough time to you since Brother Amalric left for the coast, Pagan. There's so much to do, as Commander of this house. I've commanded many forts, and Safed wasn't small, but these headquarters are quite different.' Nevertheless, he hopes I'll have the good sense and discipline to keep myself usefully employed even without his constant guidance and attention etc. etc. etc. (Pardon me while I catch up on my sleep.) Down four steps, turn right through the archway, and here's our room – with two people outside it.

One of them is Sergeant Pons, looking worried. The other is an unknown cleric – a priest, perhaps? – with a round, sweaty face.

'My lord!' Pons leaps forward. (He's a nervy type, always jumping about like a grasshopper.) 'A message, my lord! From the Patriarch!'

'It's urgent, my lord.' The cleric chimes in. 'Your presence is urgently required, by your leave. It's very important. Very important.'

Lord Roland doesn't flinch. He studies both faces, carefully, before speaking.

'Is it from the King?' he says at last. And there's something in the way he says it ... something chilly and tense and ominous.

'I don't know, my lord.' The cleric is wringing his hands. 'I don't know, I haven't heard. But I do know it's bad news. Terrible, terrible news. My lord, the Patriarch is in bed with the shock of it.' He pauses, his lips trembling. 'I think you're right, my lord. I think it's from the King.

'I think there's been a battle.'

'Brothers in Christ. As acting Commander of our Temple garrison, I have called this emergency chapter to inform you that the kingdom of Jerusalem has suffered its most terrible defeat.'

God preserve us.

'As you know, during the last month our noble King was in the northern provinces, gathering a great army. He was gathering this army to defend our kingdom against the forces of the Sultan Saladin. Several days ago, Saladin crossed the River Jordan. And in response to this challenge, our King rode out to meet him.'

A pause. Well go on. What are you waiting for? What are you waiting for? Say it, for God's sake!

'I have to tell you that he was defeated.' A quiet voice: very clear, very thin. No expression at all. 'I have to tell you

that he was captured, and many of his liege men were killed. I have to tell you that the Holy Cross is now, for this reason, in the hands of the Infidel. May God have mercy on our souls.'

There's a shaft of light falling from the window above his head. You can see the dust motes floating down, whirling around his golden hair, his wide shoulders. Everything's very still. It's as if the entire room were empty.

But it's not. That's the odd thing. It's crammed; bulging; stuffed with people. It's so full it couldn't be fuller. And Lord Roland up the front, staring down at a sea of blank faces. You can see he's trying to find the words. Very calm, though. Only his hands . . . his hands look wrong. Uncertain. Helpless.

'You will realise,' he continues, 'that many of our most valiant and pious brethren, the flower of our Order, met a noble death on this battlefield to the greater glory of God. And those who didn't fall in battle also suffered the fate of martyrs, for we have heard that they were later put to death at the hands of the Infidel. But in suffering for righteousness' sake, they suffered as our Lord Jesus Christ suffered. They died with confidence, knowing that in dying they would be delivered to the arms of Christ. For the blessed Bernard of Clairvaux has said of the Templar knight, "should he be killed himself, we know that he has not perished, but has come safely into port". And so we know that our brothers have been called to the higher glory, and are resting in the infinite love of our Lord Jesus Christ.'

A muffled noise. Sergeant Maynard has shot to his feet. Very straight and stiff. Around him, everyone's seated. Staring. The look on his face . . . wild and frantic. Ravaged. Mute. Terrible.

He draws his sword, holds it aloft. His jaw moves, but he says nothing. Just stands there. Eyes on Lord Roland. Trying to speak.

'Sit down, Brother.' Lord Roland responds, very gently. 'It's not yet time to fight. It's time to pray.'

Nothing happens. Maynard doesn't seem to hear. Suddenly Rockhead gets up, just a few rows behind. Pushes past everyone's knees. Lays a hand on Maynard's shoulder.

Can't hear what he says, but it seems to get through. The sword drops, for one thing. ('... need ... come ... help ... strong ... Brother ...') Rockhead pulls at Maynard's arm. They pick their way to the door, slowly. Not a word from Lord Roland: just a nod, as Rockhead throws him a questioning glance across the room. And the sound of their footsteps – shuffle, shuffle – as they disappear.

The silence is so heavy, it seems to force all the air from your lungs.

Only Lord Roland has the courage to break it.

'So far we've had no news about our Grand Master of the Temple. We don't know if he is alive or dead. But since it is the Rule of our Order that no ransom shall be paid for the release of any captive Templar, it is almost certain that Lord Gerard has joined our other brethren in the heavenly Kingdom of the blessed.

'Therefore, if our Grand Master is indeed dead, and since our Brother Seneschal and our Brother Marshal have also perished, the cloak of the Grand Master's authority shall fall on Brother Amalric, the Commander of these headquarters, who is now in the south as you know. From this time on we will look to Lord Amalric for directions.'

Somebody's crying. You can hear the gulps and the

snuffles. Not far away – look around – and it's Pons. His face is hidden, but his shoulders are shaking. Beside him, Gildoin. Glassy-eyed. As grey as offal.

God preserve us. I can't bear this. I just can't bear it.

'Brothers in Christ.' Lord Roland, *commanding* attention. 'Brothers in Christ these are days of tribulation for all of us here. Never before has this kingdom been under such a threat of darkness. But despite our trials, we must not lose hope. Because our Lord God has *not forsaken us.*

'You may say that such a terrible defeat is proof that we have been forsaken. Well I say that God has sent this defeat to test us in our faith, just as Job was tested. Because faith in God is *trust* in God. Many times, I have been told to consider the words of Macabees: "Victory in war is not dependent on a big army, and bravery is the gift of heaven". I now ask *you* to consider these words.

'So far as we know, Saladin has taken only one city in this kingdom. How many cities does that yet leave us? Cities full of men and women willing to defend Jerusalem with their lives, if necessary? I say to you that we may have lost the battle, but we have not yet lost the kingdom.

'Brothers in Christ, remember who you are. Remember the words of the blessed Bernard. You are the chosen troops of God. You are the valiant men of Israel. Your souls are protected by the armour of faith just as your bodies are protected by the armour of steel. How can you lose courage, knowing that you are armed with the sacred Rule of the Temple? As long as you follow the Rule, as long as you bow to its perfect discipline, rest assured that you walk in the way of salvation.'

Well I hope you're right, my lord. I certainly hope you're right. Because if you're not, we're finished.

'Praise be to God.' A voice in the crowd. 'Praise be to God for all his mercies.'

'Amen.'

'Amen.'

A chorus of pious types. All *what* mercies? Have I missed something, here? I thought we were talking about a *disaster*.

Lord Roland bows his head, briefly.

'Before we begin our prayer,' he concludes, 'I want to inform you that I shall be discussing this city's defence with the Patriarch, who of course holds authority here now in the absence of any liege lords. And I am calling a day of prayer and fasting tomorrow in honour of our fallen brethren, may their souls rest in peace, as well as a vigil tonight in the Chapel of the Cross for any of you who wish to attend.

'I now call on Father Amiel to lead us in our devotions.'

It's a peculiar feeling – like a cold wind on your heart. The fact that it's *actually happened*. It's actually happened. You live with it all your life, like a cloud on the horizon, and suddenly the storm is overhead. They've come at last, after all this time. The Infidels. Practically on the doorstep. And it's not a surprise. That's what's so awful. Everyone born here – we all knew they would come. Everyone born here is born waiting.

I don't know. It's bad enough not having a father and mother. Now I don't even have a *country* any more.

Lentils again. Terrific.

Nothing like lentils to get the old blood flowing. Boiled lentils – they really put the spark back into your spirits. The lift back into your life. Bounce back with boiled lentils! It must be the eighth time this week, surely.

There's something about the way that Fulk swings each soggy spoonful into our bowls. Splat! Like a horse depositing a load of dung. You can tell he doesn't *respect* the food. Not that there's much to admire in your average lentil. But a cook who doesn't respect his food – it makes you wonder what he's done to the stuff. (Or where it's come from, for that matter.)

Splat! Right under my nose. The scrapings of the pot, by the look of it. We always get scrapings down this end of the room. Knights' table first; then sergeants; then Turcopoles; and then, at long last, the mercenary scum. So what if the supply runs out before it reaches our bowls? We don't deserve any better.

Fulk stomps back to the kitchen to fetch the next course. Cheese, I suspect. Or crushed nuts and succory in fried cabbage rolls. Not mutton, anyway – not with everyone on rations. They promised meat or fish three times a week, and what do I get? Mutton stew on Sunday. Once upon a time they served up salt pork around here: salt pork, spiced lamb, imported beef, duck, chicken, the lot. Now everyone thinks that there's going to be a siege when Saladin comes, and they're storing all the meat with lard and salt, down in the cellars. While up here we live on chick-peas and lentils like a bunch of desert hermits.

'Let us pray.' Father Amiel at the lectern. 'Praise ye the Lord for these His blessings; praise Him for our daily bread, and all the good victuals which sustain us. Praise ye the

Lord who giveth food to all flesh, for His mercy endureth forever.'

Amen. Across the table, Odo pounces on his lentils like a leopard on a lamb. As long as it's dead, the Dungheap will eat it. I'm surprised he hasn't polished off his cutlery before now. Next to him, Arnulf. It's enough to put you off your food.

'Our reading today is from the First Book of Samuel, chapter seventeen,' Amiel announces. 'Now the Philistines gathered their armies to battle, and were gathered together at Shochoh, which belongeth to Judah, and pitched between Shochoh and Azekah, in Ephesdammim . . .'

Enter Fulk with the cheese – not a moment too soon. These lentils aren't seasoned. Not even a pinch of salt or sage. I suppose the cook knew that Lord Roland wouldn't be present, and decided not to waste his energy.

But it's an ill wind, despite everything, because Rockhead isn't too thrilled. He hasn't spoken a word (he's not allowed to) but the look on his face says it all. What, *cheese* again? And goat's cheese, at that. Scowling as he pokes at the lentil mush with his spoon. Think yourself lucky, bone-brain. There are people who'd be grateful to eat that quivering dollop. In fact there are people right here in this room who'd go down on their hands and knees just to lick it off the floor. There they are, the five of them, sitting at Lord Roland's table. Already finished. Hoping there's something more to come. The five lucky paupers who make it to every Templar meal, because charity is a Christian duty, even when supplies are running low.

You can see them lined up outside headquarters every morning, dozens of them, fighting like dogs for a spot up

the front and dressed in their filthiest tatters. Desperate for a free meal. Never the same face twice, I've noticed – at least not since I've been here. Which just goes to show what poverty there is in this city.

'...Now David was the son of that Ephrathite of Bethlehem-judah, whose name was Jesse, and he had eight sons: and the man went among men for an old man in the days of Saul...'

Odo eats like a hog. He *wallows* in his food, making the kind of noises you hear in swamps and laundries and bovine digestive systems. After eating with Odo, you spend half the day picking bits of his dinner out of your hair. Arnulf belches, loudly and richly, as Odo licks his bowl clean. It's a wonder I have any appetite at all.

And – yes! Here it comes. A pleading look from the Dungheap (otherwise known as the bottomless pit). Anything left for Odo? Not on your life, garbage guts. Time to bolt the last spoonfuls down, in case he decides to exert some force. When it's a matter of food, you can't trust Odo. Turn your back on him when he's hungry and he's likely to chew your leg off.

'...Here endeth our reading.' Amiel shuts his book with a bang: the signal for everyone to rise. You can feel the tension. One word, and the rush for the latrines will be on. Pons gives the order in Lord Roland's absence. 'Dismissed!' he says – and away they go. (Some people have no bladder control.)

The paupers file past more slowly, under the watchful eye of Sergeant Gaspard. It's his job to make sure they don't steal the cutlery. They're all grey and seedy and listless, like a mild hangover. Crawling with vermin too, by the look of

it. Limping. Coughing. Leaning heavily on sticks and crutches. But you never can tell: it might all be fakery. I've seen too many beggars who make their ulcerous sores out of oatmeal and pig's blood. Every evening Jerusalem is the scene of a thousand miracles, as blind men recover their sight, cripples recover their legs, mutes recover their voices and lepers recover their health. It's a thriving little industry, moving the hearts and milking the pockets of gullible visitors . . .

'Pagan.'

Lord Roland on the doorstep. Damn, damn, damn. Where on earth did he spring from? I thought he was discussing strategy with the Patriarch.

'Time for a sparring session before nones, I think.' He's still wearing his ceremonials: cloak, robe and ancestral sword. There's something unsettled about his forehead. 'It will only take me a moment to change.'

The shackles of duty. Trailing after him with dragging feet, my peaceful afternoon demolished. Hoping that someone will grab his attention. But they all bustle past, intent on their business. Buzz, buzz, buzz – like bees in a hive.

'Are you sure you're not too busy, my lord?' (Please, please say you are.) 'Don't feel you have to neglect others because of me. It really doesn't matter . . .'

'Of course it matters. You're going to need all the combat training I can give you before long. *Despite* what the Patriarch might think.'

Do I detect a certain crispness in his voice? It's hard to tell: someone's sharpening a blade in the armoury, and the noise is enough to make your hair stand on end. Besides which, I can't see his face.

'You mean the Patriarch actually *thinks*, my lord?' (Hurrying to catch up.) 'I couldn't be more surprised.'

'No, you're right. The Patriarch doesn't think. He prefers to dream. He doesn't want to believe that the Infidels will come. Someone else will deal with them before they reach Jerusalem. Maybe the refugees in Tyre. Or the garrison at Ascalon. Maybe the King of France will send a great army.'

'Maybe a plague of giant locusts will descend, and eat all the Saracens.'

'I'm sure he is praying for it. Meanwhile he refuses to take emergency measures. Doubtless he thinks his prayers will save us.'

Interesting. Very interesting. Lord Roland is actually *annoyed*. He's out of his cloak before he enters our room. Tossing it at me over his shoulder. Flinging open the lid of his chest. Unwrapping his swordbelt in one fluid motion.

'What emergency measures are you talking about, my lord? What won't the Patriarch do?'

'Raid the treasury. What do you think? Raid the treasury to buy food. We need food and clothes for the pilgrims trapped here. We need to open up space for refugees in the Tower of David. We need to distribute arms. That is the Master-Sergeant's decision. He *refuses* to distribute arms.'

Which doesn't surprise me. Distribute arms to the populace and our beloved Master-Sergeant's a dead man. There can't be many people in Jerusalem who wouldn't gladly fry up his liver in olive oil and mushrooms.

Lord Roland pulls his campaign tunic over his shirt. With his hair all ruffled he looks almost peevish.

'If I had the power, I'd deprive them both of their military authority,' he says. 'They are jeopardising lives with their foolishness. But what can I do? It's not my place to concern myself with these things. I am here to advise. So if they want my advice, then they should take it. Instead of wasting my time in useless chatter.' He smooths his hair, looks up, and sees my expression. The astonishment must show. It makes him twist his mouth and straighten his shoulders.

'I find them offensive,' he explains. It almost sounds like an apology. 'They are the sort of people I would like to avoid. People like that make you forget God.'

And suddenly, from the threshold, a hesitant summons. 'Lord Roland? My lord?' Rockhead peers around the door, suitably deferential. He's sweating like a piece of cheese.

'What is it, Brother?' (Frowning.) 'I'm very busy.'

'My lord, we have an absent without leave. Since first light. We ought to notify Ascalon. I believe he has family there.'

'Who? A mercenary?'

'No, my lord. He's taken his vows. Sergeant Bruno.'

A quiet hiss, like steam from a kettle. Lord Roland has never uttered a curse in his life, and apparently doesn't intend to start now. But you can tell it's an effort.

'Sergeant *Bruno*?' he says. 'The spice merchant's son? But he is such a good Templar.'

'My lord, he's taken all his equipment. And the cook reports some missing food.'

A pause. This looks promising. Lord Roland fingers the hilt of his sword.

'I have a training session now,' he murmurs. 'I'll attend to it after nones.'

'But my lord, we have the strategy chapter after nones. About the city defences.' Good old Rockhead. The inflexible man. Every appointment engraved in stone. 'And then you're inspecting the storerooms to see if they're fit for housing refugees. Remember? The Abbot of Josophat is sending a representative to advise us.'

Deliverance. Lord Roland throws a troubled glance in my direction. Time to help him out.

'It's all right, my lord. I have a lot of cleaning and polishing to do.'

Cleaning my fingernails. Polishing up my collection of dirty jokes. I mean, why kill yourself working? We'll all be dead soon enough.

'My lord?' Sergeant Pons arrives on the doorstep. 'My lord, we have to organise the next watch bill –'

'Yes, yes, I'm coming.' It's practically a snarl. Practically, but not quite.

One of these days, before we all lay down our arms and face the judgement seat, I'm going to see Lord Roland lose his temper.

Chapter 5

The Palace of the Patriarchs. Not much to look at, from the street. A towering block of dung-brown stone, heavily fortified, no flags or banners, just two or three arched windows high up on the second storey. And a cavernous entrance punched through the eastern wall, opposite the Church of the Holy Sepulchre.

Solid workmanship is the best you can say for it.

Never set foot inside, myself, though I've passed it often enough. Don't much care for the neighbourhood, personally. Wedged between the grain market and the Postern of Saint Lazarus: between a floating mist of chaff and the stink of decaying lepers (huddled around the postern like flies around an open wound). Either way, you can hardly breathe. And the smell hasn't improved since I

was last in the area. In fact there seems to be more dung on the street – unless I'm imagining things.

You forget what it's like out here, when you're living in Templar headquarters. You forget that people out here aren't forced to scrub the pavement with lime when they piss on it.

'Make way! Make way! Out of the way, woman!' A palace guard, beating through the doleful crowds on the doorstep. *They're* new, as well. Never seen *them* before. Not beggars, either: most of them are quite well dressed, in rain capes and lamb's wool and embroidered money pouches. Hugging their bags and bundles, nursing listless children on their knees. At a guess, I'd say they were stranded pilgrims. Stranded pilgrims waiting for help.

Lord Roland catches my eye as they shuffle apart to let us through. He obviously doesn't like it.

'Pagan.' (Softly.) 'Does that child look ill to you?'

'I don't know, my lord.' Who do you think I am – Brother Gavin? Doesn't look too bad. Doesn't look too good, either. 'Do you want me to ask anyone?'

'No, no. I'll take it up with the Patriarch.'

On through the gate and into the courtyard, which is paved with stone and deep as a well. Shadowy doorways lead off in all directions. Bales of straw. A broken cartwheel. And stretched out on an empty barrel to dry, somebody's quilted corselet. Most of the guards are wearing them. Used to wear one myself, on night patrol. The poor man's armour: two flimsy layers of linen stuffed with flax. A single downpour and you spend the rest of your life trying to dry it out.

'You there!' Lord Roland's 'patrician' voice. Crisp, confident, imperious. Used only on special occasions. 'We

have a meeting with the Patriarch. We are expected.' The usual rapid response, as the guard ushers us both through one of the doorways. Beyond it, a stairwell drenched in urine. Delightful. A stink so bad it practically dissolves your teeth at fifty paces. Haven't smelt anything this ferocious since Odo last took off his boots.

Lord Roland, of course, doesn't twitch a nostril. Pursues the guard at a leisurely pace, like someone who wouldn't know an urgent summons if he was married to it. Just passing through, you know. Thought I'd drop in – catch up on the gossip . . . And suddenly there's carpet underfoot. Rich woollen carpet, straight from Damascus. Tapestries on the walls. Flickering silken scenes, weaving and swaying as stray draughts punch at their backs.

We turn left . . . left again . . . through a big carved door . . . and stop.

Behold the Patriarch.

'Lord Roland! Praise God. We've been waiting this last hour. Welcome, my lord, you must hear this, come in. Who's that? Your squire? Come in . . .'

When did I last see him? Easter before last, I think, in the Church of the Holy Sepulchre. He looks about the same. Not your typical career cleric. Most of *them* are running to fat, but this one's kept his figure. Tall, slim and supple; narrow shoulders; long neck; face that launched a thousand fantasies. The Lily of the Auvergne, they call him. Frankish, of course. Eyes like sapphires and lashes as long as your arm. No brain to speak of, but who needs a brain when you've got the kind of brawn that appeals to women of influence? Everyone knows that he wooed his way to the top.

Beside him, the Master-Sergeant. God preserve us. One glance, and he looks away.

I don't recognise the other man.

'You know the Master-Sergeant, of course. And this is Ernio of the Mallone. A merchant from Acre.' The Lily waves a graceful hand, studded with badly chewed fingernails. 'He's brought us news from the north. Tell Lord Roland what you just told me, Master Mallon.'

'My lord.' The merchant bows. He's a chunky, careful, grey-headed Venetian. The sort of man you generally never see without his samples, account books, and brother-in-law. But he doesn't look well. His eyes are bloodshot, his colour is bad. There's a greasy shine to his complexion. 'My lord,' he says, 'Acre has surrendered. Saladin has occupied the city. The Seneschal offered it in exchange for all lives and possessions ten days ago –'

'And now Saladin has moved north,' the Lily breaks in. 'North and east, into Galilee and Samaria. But Tyre has held out. As I said it would.' No prize for guessing what *he* thinks. This supports his argument for doing damn-all. Lord Roland frowns.

'Was there *no* defence at Acre? No fighting?'

'No, my lord. I think they lost heart, when they saw the King held captive. He was there himself.' A pause, as the merchant plucks up his courage. 'And so was your Grand Master, my lord. The Grand Master of the Templars.'

'*What?*'

'They were both there. I saw them, before we left.'

Well, well, well. Here's a puzzle. The first Grand Master to survive captivity for more than a day. Theoretically, he's

supposed to be a waste of space – because you can't ransom a Templar. So why has Saladin kept him alive?

'We should send for reinforcements from the south,' says the Lily, 'while the Infidels are still in the north. We should bring in troops from Gaza to defend us.'

'But if Gaza sends troops, who will defend Gaza?' says Lord Roland. 'You should remember that Egypt lies to the south, your grace. In Gaza they have problems of their own.'

The voice of reason. But he sounds preoccupied, as if he's wrestling with a private concern. The Lily begins to gnaw at a thumbnail.

'Gaza is nothing,' he whines. 'Gaza is not the holy city. They *must* send troops, when they hear we are threatened.' (To the merchant.) 'How many of you have come from Acre? Did you bring your possessions with you?'

'We brought what we could carry, your grace. The rest has gone to Saladin.'

'Ah.'

A short and gloomy silence. Call this a strategic conference? I've seen smarter tactics in a drunkard trying to negotiate his way down a flight of stairs. Lord Roland addresses the merchant as Heraclius spits a fragment of thumbnail onto the carpet.

'Those people at the palace gate. Have they also come from Acre with you?'

'Yes, my lord.'

'And have they not been given shelter?'

'It's all in hand,' the Lily snaps. What a sepulchre-head. Somewhere in the building a bell tolls, and he uncoils himself in response. 'I'll have to leave now, but we can

discuss this tomorrow,' he says. 'Thank you, Lord Roland. Thank you, Master Mallon. That will be all.'

What a pus-bag. What a prize boil. He struts out the door like a peacock, trailing half a mile of iridescent plumage behind him. Probably gone off to meet his latest girlfriend. Meanwhile, the merchant's been dropped like a dismembered limb. Standing there with his jaw dangling around his knees. Lord Roland's about to take pity (I can tell), but old Garlic-Breath the Master-Sergeant forestalls him. 'Can I have a word with you, my lord?' he says. 'In private?' I don't like the look of this at all.

I don't like the way he's ignored my very existence from the moment I walked in the room. Standing there silent, with his hairy arms folded and his balding head bowed.

'Wait for me outside, Pagan. I won't be long.'

So the merchant and I end up on the doorstep, like bags of kitchen garbage. He wanders off a broken man, and I'm left to count my fingernails. Wondering what the Master-Sergeant could possibly be up to. Knew that I shouldn't have come on this jaunt. Knew that I'd run into trouble. But what can you do? I mean, orders are orders.

Can't hear anything – not a single word. Not even with my ear to the door. What does that pig's liver think he's doing? He can't arrest me. Lord Roland outranks him.

'Yes, my lord. Thank you, my lord . . .'

Pulling away as the door swings open. Who, me? Eavesdropping? Never. Lord Roland strides out with a flick of his cape, followed by Garlic-Breath, who's bowing and scraping. The very picture of humility. A moment to treasure.

'Come, Pagan. It's time for us to leave.'

And away we go, without a word of farewell. Turn right. Right again. Down the hall and hit the stairs. Holding my breath (and my nose) until we're clear of the stink and standing in the courtyard.

'My lord?'

'Yes, Pagan.'

'What did he say? The Master-Sergeant?'

'He said you were a thief. A thief, a liar, a blasphemer, a sluggard, a gamester and a consumer of strong drink. Just in case I didn't know.'

Hmmm.

'And what did *you* say, my lord?'

'I said: "He that is without sin among you, let him first cast a stone".'

Lord Roland passes judgement, and the world obeys. He looks at me for a moment – just one look – and moves to grab old Coppertail's bridle. You can practically see the halo shining above his head.

Outside the gates, the refugees are still waiting.

94

It's very dark, but I know where I am. I'm lying in bed, and the bed is wet. I can feel it beneath me. It's not my bed, though. My bed's in the corner. This *can't* be my bed.

Everyone else is asleep. They're all safe asleep, and they can't help me. They wouldn't help me anyway. I can see the door open. I can see him, Father Benedict, holding his stick. But I can't see his face, because I'm hiding under the blanket. If I keep very still, very quiet, if I try and try, perhaps I'll disappear, and he won't be able to see me.

He's stopping at each bed, one by one. There are so many beds: perhaps the bell will ring before he reaches mine. But he moves so fast from bed to bed. Perhaps they're empty after all. But they can't be. They can't be. No one has ever run away because they'll catch you, and put you down the bottom of a deep, dark well. Perhaps he's killing them. God, please help me. Please help me, God. He's coming closer . . . closer . . .

I'm very still. Very still. Don't breathe. But he knows what I'm doing. He knows my bed is wet. He knows everything. He always says so. He leans down, down, closer and closer, wheezing through his pointed teeth, he's going to – he's going to –

No! No! He's going to *kill* me!

'Pagan.'

It's dark. I can't see. But I'm awake now: I know I am. Because that was Lord Roland's voice.

'Pagan? Are you all right?'

Oh dear. I must have said something.

'I'm sorry, my lord. Did I wake you?'

'I was awake already. Was it a bad dream? You shouted.'

Father Benedict. It feels as if he's still in the room. I almost wish he was, so I could skewer his guts and stamp on his face and chop off his arms and make him eat them.

Why can't they leave me alone? After all these years? They must be dead by now, most of them. Perhaps they've come back to haunt me.

'Yes, my lord. It was a bad dream.'

'I've been having bad dreams too, these last few nights.' A surprising revelation from out of the darkness. 'Full of

bloody faces and weeping children. I hope it's not a bad omen. What was *your* dream about?'

'Oh – nothing apocalyptic, my lord. Nothing to do with Jerusalem. It was a childish dream. Mad.'

'Most of them are. Do you mean to say that you dreamed about being a child again?'

Now that's very sharp. How on earth did he know that?

'Yes, my lord. Alas.'

Long silence. But somehow – don't ask me why – I know that he hasn't dozed off. What *is* he doing, lying awake at this hour? It seems so out of character.

'When did you leave your monastery, Pagan?'

'Saint Joseph's?' (What's that got to do with anything?) 'I left when I was ten, my lord. Praise God.'

'And when did you first enter it?'

'When I was two days old. Or so they say. Can't remember the occasion, myself.'

'So you never knew your parents.'

'Well – I never knew my father. Neither did my mother. He came and went like an attack of swamp belly.'

Pause.

'What?' Completely baffled. 'What on earth do you mean?'

'He was a brigand, my lord. Passing through her village. She never knew his name.' (If he even had one, the animal.) 'She gave me this name herself. Only thing she ever did give me.'

'That's not entirely true, Pagan. She gave you your life, after all.'

Oh yes. My life. And one terrific gift *that* was.

Sometimes I think that I would have done better without it.

'I don't know if that was a gift, my lord. More like an accident.'

Outside, many miles away, a dog howls. Amazing how quiet it is. Only a gust of wind now and then, as if the whole city were empty. Empty and desolate. It used to be that way sometimes on night patrol, when there were no children crying or cats fighting, and when your lantern went 'clink, clink' as you walked along.

Cheery.

'Did you run away from your monastery, Pagan?'

'Yes, my lord. As soon as possible.'

'I thought as much.' Somewhere in the darkness his brain is turning, round and round like a water-wheel. 'They wouldn't have taught you to read if they hadn't intended to keep you. So you didn't like it, then.'

'No, my lord.' (Understatement of the year.) 'I didn't.'

'Why not?'

Why not? Dry bread and water. Marching in straight lines. No talking between sunset and dawn. No talking in the cloister. No talking at meals. No leaving the monastery grounds without permission. No running. No shouting. No laughing. No wetting the bed.

Father Benedict, with his hard wooden cane, and his ugly mouth, and his silent beatings.

Blood on the blankets.

Why *not*?

'No girls, my lord. And no jokes, either.'

Another long silence. Not so much as a rustle. Wonder what time it is? Must be very early. Probably an hour or so to

matins. Still enough of the night left to get a reasonable amount of sleep . . .

'I've been thinking about you, Pagan.'

God preserve us. Here's trouble.

'I've been thinking that I have never met anyone like you before. And I think I understand why, now. It seems to me that you have been given only one thing in your entire life, and that is your education. No saint gave you his name, so you have no saint's day. No family. No property. No place in the world. And no loving friends to watch over you, unless I'm mistaken. You have nothing except your learning. But most people with nothing don't even have that. So I think your learning is what makes you so different.'

Different in what way? Don't know if I want to ask.

'My lord, with all respect, you shouldn't take my learning too seriously. It might look impressive to be able to read, but that's because you can't read yourself. When you learn to read, all you can do is read. It doesn't change anything.'

'No, Pagan. You're wrong. I'm quite sure you're wrong. Because people who read, they are always – they are always a little like you.' He thinks for a moment. 'You can't just tell them. You have to tell them *why.*'

Clear as mud.

'I don't understand, my lord. Are you saying that's a good thing or a bad thing?'

'I don't know. I used to think it was a bad thing. It can be very dangerous. But now I don't know . . .'

All at once it's hard to concentrate. He's speaking very softly, and his voice is like the sound of doves cooing. Like a gentle wind in the treetops. Like Father Arniel

droning on through the Book of Numbers, chapter twenty-six.

Yawn.

'But what I want to say to you, Pagan, is that you're not like me.' (No. Really? What a revelation.) 'All my life God has showered me with blessings. Because of His infinite love, the people around me have bestowed on me all manner of gifts. So my purpose in life is to ask: what can I do to repay my benefactors? How can I use this fortunate life of mine to the benefit of others?

'But you have been given nothing – or next to nothing. So you owe nothing to anyone but yourself. You are free to build your own life, to your own advantage.

'Pagan? Do you understand me? I'm saying that in giving you nothing else, God has given you the gift of freedom. And that is a very precious gift.

'Pagan? Are you listening?'

'Yes, my lord . . . freedom . . . right . . .' (Yawn.)

'Think about it.'

Think about it. Sure. Think about it tomorrow. Tomorrow. There's a special service on, tomorrow. Prayers for deliverance – Church of the Holy Sepulchre. Have to be there, bright and early. Have to be there. Bright and early, with a clear head.

Have to get some sleep . . .

It must be the greatest church in the world. Massive dome, marble floor, golden mosaics, pillars like the legs of giants, three-storeyed walls, jewelled lamps, silver-gilt trimmings, prophets on the vault, everything.

Trouble is, it's always full of pilgrims. Or priests. Or hundreds and hundreds of noisy, filthy, stinking, fighting, sweating, brainless, vicious, uncontrollable worshippers.

'Well?'

Rockhead's arrived: God knows how he managed to force his way through the multitudes. By punching little old ladies' heads in, probably.

'It's a mess out there, my lord.' (Gasping.) 'The crowds – they're piled up as far as the abbey. Thousands of them. And they're all trying to get in here.'

'I see.'

Lord Roland surveys the situation. Cretins to the left of him, cretins to the right. Standing head and shoulders above them all, like a cedar in a bed of parsley. The Patriarch still hasn't appeared.

'This has to be dealt with,' he says. 'We can't let this go on. I want you and Pagan on the door, sergeant. I don't want any more people coming in. You can threaten them, if you have to.'

My pleasure. Following Rockhead as he pushes his way to the door. Squeezing past great slabs of hot, sticky flesh, through steamy clouds of garlic and onions and spice and sweat and hot peppers. Whoof! What a stew! Rockhead uses his elbows, his knees, his shoulders, his fists. Yelps and squeaks from the targets. Then into the sunshine – and a sea of heads stretching out across the square.

Christ in a cream cheese sauce.

'Attention! *Attention!*' Rockhead, the man with a voice like the fall of Jericho, can hardly be heard above the clamour – until he raises his spear. 'Attention, citizens! *Attention!* The church is full! There is *no more room!* Please remain where you are!'

Ominous mutterings, swelling to outrage. The bodies surge forward. Funny how you only see bits of them: a sagging bosom, a straining forearm, a mouthful of greenish, jagged teeth. One quick nod from Rockhead, and out with my sword.

Whoops! That's done it. They can't fall back fast enough.

'If you force your way into the church the people inside may suffer injury!' Rockhead declares, trying to appeal to their better natures. Pointless, of course. When the going gets tough, there's no such thing as a better nature – not in large and pious groups of people.

Personally, I can't see what all the fuss is about. So we'll miss the Patriarch's new outfit. So what? More like a blessing than a curse, if you ask me.

'Quiet! Quiet!' Voice from the crowd. 'It has begun! Quiet, everyone!'

Sure enough, the choir's started. You can hear the singing, even from out here. '*Laudamus te, adoramus te . . .*' Chins sink obediently onto chests. A general easing of the noise, as the keener souls resign themselves to a beggar's seat near the doorstep. Some arrange themselves on the ground, some lean against the limestone walls of the square, fanning themselves with their gauntlets. Some remain standing, heads bowed, hands clasped. And the flies settle down for a nice, long feed.

Is there anyone out there I recognise?

No . . . no . . . no. Not him. Not him, either. A tangle of greasy grey hair, like a dirty goat's fleece. (No.) The face beside it – sallow and bony and pocked. (No.) To the right, an enormous black beard. To the left, a saffron silk turban

over a pair of high cheekbones. A cloven chin. (No.) A missing eye. (No.) A smooth, flushed cheek just peeping out of a collar. Very nice. Very nice indeed. Lovely, the way these northern women dress. No veils. No shrouds. No layers and layers of clothing. Lots of lovely bare skin and hair, for all the world to see.

Better watch it, though, or she's going to get sunburned. In fact we're *all* heading for a dose of sunburn, in this heat. The hoods are a good idea. Someone pulling his cloak over his head . . . And who's that big, brown baldie beside him? Looks like Oswald the ostler. No. It can't be. No – it's not. Didn't think so. Last thing I heard old Oswald had run off to Nazareth. After the unfortunate affair of the borrowed donkey.

Ho hum.

'Let God arise, let his enemies be scattered: let them also that hate him flee before him.'

The Patriarch's voice. Quite clear, surprisingly. Drifting out of the church like a wisp of smoke. Like the insidious smell of chicken manure. High and thin and strained. Not the kind of voice to reassure you in the face of bloodthirsty Infidel armies. Not exactly the ringing tones you'd expect. Makes you wonder if God will even *hear* him, let alone deliver us all from the raging heathen.

We'd be better off at home, if you ask me. Packing our clothes and pots and jewellery and a spare pair of boots.

'. . . Because of thy temple at Jerusalem shall kings bring presents unto thee. Rebuke the company of spearmen . . . scatter thou the people that delight in war . . . strength unto God . . . thou art terrible out of thy holy places . . .'

A slight commotion. Scuffling feet; urgent voices; milling crowds behind us on the porch. A tight knot of people bursts from the shadows, demanding air, light, water, fire, help, anything. There's a woman suspended between them, limp as a rag. Fainted, by the look of it.

'Make way! Make way!'

'A priest! Get a priest!'

'She needs fanning! Somebody get a fan!'

'Is she all right? What happened?'

About five thousand people press forward to have a look. Rockhead waves them back with his spear as someone – a relative? – succumbs to hysteria. You have to admit, the victim doesn't look too well. Her face is the colour of raw tripe.

Heatstroke, probably. It's like an oven inside that church.

'Where does she live?' (Rockhead.) 'Does anyone know where she lives?'

'She lives with him.'

'I am her son. Her only son . . .'

'Right.' Looking around for Inc. 'Kidrouk. You stay here. We need an armed escort on this one, or they'll never get through the crowds. Hold your position. I won't be long.' (To the weeping relation.) 'Calm down, she's not dead.' (To the white-faced son.) 'We'll take her home – or do you want to stop at Saint John's hospital? It's only around the corner.'

'I don't . . . I don't know . . .'

'Sergeant?' Loudly, so he can hear me over the rabble. 'Lord Roland says the hospital is full to bursting with sick refugees. He said so yesterday. It might not be a good idea –'

'Home, then. Come on. And *stay behind my back.*'

One thing you can say for old Rockhead – he certainly knows how to handle a crowd. It's like watching Moses part the Red Sea, only Rockhead has to get in there and do it with his elbows. Straight through the middle, no 'pleases' or 'pardons', with the sick woman's escort bringing up the rear. Quite fast, considering. And the bodies surge together again behind them.

'. . . They that trust in the Lord shall be as Mount Sion, which cannot be removed, but abideth forever. As the mountains are round about Jerusalem, so the Lord is round about his people . . .'

The Patriarch, still droning on. Wonder if he's noticed that his congregation is passing out from sheer boredom? Or maybe it isn't boredom. Maybe it's just his bad breath.

Everyone's more interested in the victim now, anyway. Discussing her departure in low, respectful voices. Craning their necks to catch a glimpse of Rockhead's upraised spearhead as it lurches out of sight.

Yawn, yawn, yawn. I wonder how much longer?

'*Jerusalem hath grievously sinned!*'

Christ in a cream cheese sauce.

'*Jerusalem hath grievously sinned, therefore all that honoured her despise her! Her enemies prosper, for the Lord hath afflicted her for the multitude of her transgressions!*'

God preserve us. A voice like fifty thousand fruit pedlars screaming in unison.

But where is it coming from?

'*The adversary hath spread out his hand on all her pleasant things, for she hath seen that the heathen entered into her sanctuary!*'

There he is. A tiny old man. A tiny old man the size of a grain sack, with a beard like the drifting cobwebs you find in stables – full of fleas and straw and dried dung. A tiny old madman, all waving hands and staring eyes.

The sort of tiny old madman who isn't going to shut up and sit still unless I knock him unconscious with something blunt and heavy.

I mean, wouldn't you know it? Left in command for the space of two heartbeats and *this* has to happen!

Chapter 6

'Let us lift up our hearts unto God in the heavens! We have transgressed and have rebelled! Fear and a snare is come upon us, desolation and destruction!'

'Be quiet!'

'Our end is near, our days are fulfilled, for our end is come!'

'Shut up!'

'Push off!'

'The punishment of thine iniquity is accomplished, O daughter of Sion!'

The Patriarch's puny warble doesn't stand a chance. Not against *this* mighty tide of sound. Pure, unbridled, skull-cracking sound. Such a big noise to come out of such a little old man. It's uncanny.

So what should I do? Should I drag him off ? Knock him out? Shout him down? (Impossible.) He doesn't look

very tough, but you never can tell with these maniacs. He might have the strength of Samson's big brother.

If I don't do something soon there's going to be a fight. That's obvious enough from the hisses. And the shouts. And the fruit stones bouncing off his naked skull. Perhaps I should turn my back and let them do their own dirty work.

But what's this? Oh dear. Support from the spectators.

'It's true! It's true what he says! Jerusalem has sinned with the heathen, and now we'll *all* be punished!'

A tall young foreigner. You can tell he's a foreigner: the clipped beard, the fresh, white skin, the dull, muddy clothes on his back. Why do foreigners always dress as if they dye their clothes with vegetable scraps and store them in peat bogs? He has that red-eyed, raw-nerved, wild look – the look you see on penitent pilgrims staggering out of the drinking shops at dawn.

'Jerusalem has sinned! You are all sinners! You wear heathen costume and eat heathen foods and take baths and shut up your women like Infidels! You even *trade* with the heathen! And now God has punished us all for your sins!'

God help us. That's done it. A gigantic slab of solid gristle shoots to its feet, as taut as a bowstring. Red-faced with rage. Deeply offended.

'Sins?' it roars. 'What sins? You'd better shut your festering mouth, my friend, or I'll damn well shut it for you!'

Nicely put, but it's pointless. The foreigner just ploughs on. Doesn't even realise he's risking a mouthful of knucklebone.

'This is supposed to be a holy city, but look at it! Look at it! It's a sink of vice! A pit full of thieves and cut-throats and whited sepulchres – !'

'Are you calling me a *thief*?'

All right. Enough's enough. If I don't do something now, I'm going to get a kick up the backside for letting five thousand innocent churchgoers spill each other's brains all over the steps of the Holiest of Holies.

But what the hell can I do?

'Citizens! *Citizens!* People of Jerusalem!'

Nobody blinks an eyelid. I might as well not be here. Time for the Kidrouk double-strength bone-breaker street alarm whistle. Guaranteed to burst eyeballs and shake the fleas out of a dog's coat at fifty paces.

'Twe-e-e-e-e-e-e-ep!'

Whoops! That's done it. You can practically see the hairs leap from their scalps and run for cover.

'Citizens! You're missing the Patriarch's prayer –'

'The Patriarch is a hypocrite too!' (Christ in a cream cheese sauce. God curse that loud-mouthed foreigner.) 'The Patriarch's sins have brought this punishment upon us! He is the natural product of a corrupt and evil den of vile iniquity!'

'Well of course he is. He was born in France. But that's not *our* fault, you know.'

Laughter from the locals. I wish I hadn't said that. It wasn't a smart thing to do.

And sure enough, here comes the backlash. The backlash from France – broad, blonde and oozing out of his breeches.

'*What did you say?*'

'He said that Frenchmen were all hatched from the same dung-heap!' A loud vote of confidence from the dough-faced creature with a voice like someone squeezing air from

a wineskin. 'Didn't you hear? Or are you deaf as well as dimwitted?'

The Frenchman turns and knocks him flat.

Whump! Instant chaos. Fists flying. Women screaming. Someone banging someone else's head on the ground.

Good job, Pagan. Nice work. Marvellous.

'Oi! Hey! Get off him!' Go for the Frenchman. Pushed away – try again – grip on the arm – *wham* in the breastbone.

Ow ... ow ... help. This is awful. Sword out. Pointless. Wave it around? Use the hilt? Stop this, for God's sake! Somebody help me ...

'*What on earth is going on?*'

Lord Roland.

High on the steps, gleaming white, not very happy. Like a mother who's found her children piddling on her newly washed bedclothes.

Amazing what an impact he can have. Tempers cool. Voices falter. People release their grip on other people's facial hair.

'Pagan?'

'Yes – yes, my lord –' (Coughing.)

'Where is Sergeant Tibald?'

'He went – he had to escort the sick lady home ...'

Sobs from the tub of lard on the pavement. Blood all over his face and hands.

Broken nose, by the look of it.

'This is disgraceful.' Lord Roland's most ominous tones. 'Disgraceful.'

'*He* started it!' (A shrill female voice.) 'It's the foreigner's fault!' But the Man of Marble doesn't bow to popular prejudice. He's above all that.

'Brawling on the steps of our most holy place,' he says. 'There is no excuse for such behaviour. It will lose us the kingdom.' Raising his voice. 'I am shocked! I am shocked to the heart that you should stoop to such low and vicious acts. You came to pray, not to fight. If you call yourselves Christians you should kneel and ask forgiveness for this disgraceful exhibition, or leave these sacred precincts now!'

Will they or won't they? Yes, that's done it. Down they go. Slowly, unwillingly, muttering into their folded hands. And Lord Roland standing up there like the Last Judgement, stony-faced.

He throws me a look. You too, Pagan.

Christ in a cream cheese sauce.

'O Jerusalem, wash thine heart from wickedness that thou mayest be saved! How long shall thy vain thoughts lodge within thee?'

The madman. Clearly visible over the heads of the kneeling multitudes. Lost in his own obsession.

'That's him, my lord.' (Quietly, tugging at the cloak I just washed last week.) 'That's where the trouble started.'

A nod.

'I couldn't march him out, my lord, because there weren't enough men for an escort –'

'It doesn't matter.' To the madman. 'You! Old fellow! What is your name?'

A brief silence. The lunatic looks startled – confused. His voice drops to a normal register. 'I speak the lamentations of Jeremiah the prophet,' he says.

'Very well, Jeremiah. It is time to pray. We are praying to the Lord for His forgiveness. Will you kneel and join us, please?'

And damn me – he does it. The madman actually does it. Falling to his knees without a word of protest. Meek as a lamb.

Lord Roland the miracle worker.

'. . . The Lord is my light and my salvation; whom shall I fear? The Lord is the strength of my life; of whom shall I be afraid? . . .' The Patriarch's voice, audible once more in the stillness. Lord Roland bows his head. Piety reigns. The air's so thick with it you could practically bottle the stuff and sell it to pilgrims.

But who's that across the square? A Templar sergeant. Rockhead? No. Gildoin.

'My lord . . .'

A gentle nudge, and Lord Roland raises his eyes. Sees Gildoin, who makes the sign of the trumpet. Some kind of message. An important message.

Bad news, I'll bet.

'. . . Though a host should encamp against me, my heart shall not fear. Though war should rise against me, in this will I be confident . . .'

Watching old Gildoin pick his way between the tightly packed bodies. Sliding and squeezing and burrowing. Quite a different approach from Rockhead's. Less forceful. More flexible. But then he *is* a lot smaller.

The approach of the little, leathery face, as dry and wrinkled as a dusty peach stone. Eyes like chips of jade. Mouth like a panther trap.

No expression whatsoever.

'Well?' (Lord Roland.) 'Quietly, please.'

'My lord, there's a messenger from Ascalon . . .'

'Yes?'

'My lord . . .' Gildoin licks his withered lips. 'My lord, Jaffa has fallen.'

What?

Oh no. You can't be serious. You can't be. It's impossible.

Lord Roland takes a deep breath.

'Who?' he says. 'Not Saladin.'

'No, my lord, it was Saladin's brother, al-Adil. He came up from Egypt, past Ascalon. Jaffa –'

'Is not so well defended. Of course.'

'My lord, there were no terms. He stormed the city.'

And we all know what *that* means. Wholesale bloodshed. God preserve us.

Al-Adil, not seventeen parasangs away.

'. . . Wait on the Lord, be of good courage, and he shall strengthen thine heart.' The Patriarch's drone. 'Wait, I say, on the Lord. Amen.'

'Amen.' A gentle echo from the kneeling multitudes. Briefly, expressively, Lord Roland closes his eyes.

God and all the saints preserve us.

'Ascalon has fallen.'

'What . . .?'

'Ascalon has fallen. Ascalon and Gaza.'

Bonetus, flitting past like a puff of wind. Grab him or he'll disappear.

'Wait! Stop! Tell me . . .'

He looks strange – fierce – his brown eyes burning in his face. Sweat gleaming on his cheekbones. Blood pulsing under his skin.

Breathless.

'You want to know what happened?' he pants. 'I'll tell you. Saladin came to the city walls with the King. The King and our Grand Master. Both of them pleaded for Ascalon to submit.'

'*What?*'

'Wait, just wait. It gets better. When the city refused to submit, it was stormed, and our noble Grand Master sent word to Gaza ordering our knights there to lay down their arms. Oh yes. And they did it too. Because these were *orders*, you know. Orders from the Grand Master. It's against the *Rule* to disobey!'

Christ in a cream cheese sauce. This is unbelievable.

'Who told you?'

'Who told me? Hah! Who told me? I'll tell you who told me!' (Is he going a little mad, I wonder?) 'There are *some* Templars who don't take orders from Gerard-de-Craven-Ridfort, Grand Master or not! They shouldered their weapons and escaped from Gaza to fight the Infidels even if it cost them their lives! *They* don't let the fear of death come between them and their solemn vows! *They* don't play games of ransom with the Holy Land! They're going to stand and fight to their *last drop of blood!*'

He's so angry it's frightening. Any moment now his brain is going to burst out of his ears.

'But if there were orders – ?'

'*Damn* the orders! We'll fight *without* orders!'

And off he goes – whoosh! – like a stone from a catapult. Singeing the leather on his boots.

Off to spread the word, probably. Wonder who escaped from Gaza? Wonder if it's anyone I know? They must have

turned up just now . . . gone straight to Lord Roland. Odd that he hasn't called a chapter to announce the news.

Perhaps I should report for duty. Old Coppertail can miss her rubdown, for once.

'You don't mind, do you sweetheart?'

A snort from the biting end. This mare doesn't like me.

'Pagan?'

Sigebert the Saxon. He must have been down in Walnut's stall, fanning the flies away. They ought to move his bed in there and have done with it.

'Oh. Hello, Sig.'

'Did he say that *Ascalon* has fallen? Did he?'

'Ascalon and Gaza.'

'Oh *no!*'

He goggles like a stranded fish. Pale, weedy and bloodless; red-rimmed eyes, soapy skin, scabs all over his face and body. One of those people you avoid like the plague.

'What are we going to do?' he says.

'We're going to do what we're told.' (Gathering up my combs and brushes.) 'The way we always do.'

'Where are you going?'

'I'm off to find Lord Roland. I think he's upstairs somewhere.'

'Can I come too?'

God preserve us. No thanks.

'You'd better stay here, Sig, you've got a sick horse to look after. Sergeant Tibald will fry your guts if she dies when you're not around.'

Poor old Sigebert. What a hopeless case. One of those people who make hardened warriors shudder: who can

empty a room as fast as a bad smell. When Saladin arrives we should send Sigebert out to meet him. One hour of Sigebert and he'll be heading back to Damascus as fast as his legs can carry him.

The stairs are empty: Bonetus must have been and gone. First stop, the chapter hall. No one inside. Maynard is sitting near the refectory, staring at the ground. Keep clear of *him*. He's been in an odd mood, lately. Around the corner, turn left, and here are the kitchens. Out of bounds. Still no one in sight. Perhaps the latrines . . .? It can be nice and cool in there, on a hot day.

Gildoin is sitting over the sluice drain, lost in thought.

'Excuse me, sergeant.'

He looks up.

'Would you know where I can find Lord Roland?'

It takes a while for the question to sink in.

'Lord Roland?' Vaguely. 'No, I don't. Maybe the Undermarshal . . .'

Maybe the Undermarshal's office. Stop at the armoury, just in case. There's a cluster of brown tunics near the door: Welf, Gaspard, Gavin. They look anxious and confused.

'. . . I never trusted him. I always said so, didn't I? I always said he had the heart of a mercenary.' (Gaspard.) 'Flemings are all the same.'

'He's a politician, pure and simple.' Gavin's twitching like a fly on a fish-hook. I've never seen him so fired up. The sparks are practically shooting from his beard. 'He came to the Holy Land to seek his fortune, not to fight for God.'

'Wasn't he in Raymond of Tripoli's service?'

'That's right. And do you know why he left? Because Raymond promised him an heiress – the first available – and then broke his promise. That's why Gerard joined the Order. Because he missed out on marrying an heiress. He was never a *true* Templar.'

'May God strike him down for his sinfulness.'

Obviously discussing our beloved Grand Master's treachery. (I didn't know about the heiress.)

'What is it, Kidrouk?'

'Please, sir, I'm looking for Lord Roland.'

'Well he's not here. I think he's with Sergeant Tibald. In the Draper's office.'

Gavin protests.

'But I thought they were in the council room?'

'No, he's with Sergeant Pons.' (Gaspard.) 'I'm sure he is . . .'

No help *there*. Thanks for nothing. On past Rockhead's locked door. This is all very strange – very disorganised. Turn left to reach the Undermarshal's office. There are voices coming from inside.

Knock, knock.

'Who is it?'

Rockhead's familiar bark. He jerks the door open. There's a strange knight standing behind him: very young, very dirty, with big brown eyes and no beard.

Must be one of the escapees from Gaza.

'Well?'

'I'm – I'm looking for Lord Roland –'

'Ask Sergeant Pons.'

Bang! The door slams shut in my face. Such courtesy. And where now, I wonder? The council room? The Draper's

office? The chapel, maybe? That's an idea. Perhaps Lord Roland's praying for guidance. It's the sort of thing he would do.

Back across the courtyard. That knight looked interesting. No beard... must be new to the Order. Probably an idealist. Wonder if he brought anyone else along? Certainly hope so. We need all the help we can get.

Turn a corner, and wham! Sergeant Pons.

'Kidrouk! Have you seen Lord Roland? No? Damn it!'

And away he goes.

What is *happening* here? I don't like this. I don't like it at all.

Might as well check the chapel. The door's open, anyway. Candles burning on the altar. Cool, dim, quiet. A long, high room with an arched ceiling, very simple, no dark little side chapels or clusters of columns or big marble tombs to hide behind.

Nobody here.

Well that's it, then. It's a mystery to me. Unless he's gone back to our room? Oh no – Pons would have looked *there*, surely.

Still. It's worth a try.

Passing Bonetus on the way back to the western wing. He's busy breaking the news to Father Amiel – probably scaring him half to death. Odd that he's roaming around like this. Why hasn't Lord Roland called a special chapter? That's what I want to know.

The door to our room: shut, as usual. Better knock. Just to be on the safe side.

No response.

Give it a push – peer in – look around.

Lord Roland is slumped on the floor in one corner.

'My lord!'

Oh God. He's dead. No – he's sick. His wound! His scar's burst.

'My lord! What's wrong?! Are you ill? Is it your wound? What is it?'

I've never seen him so pale. His eyes open ... close ... his skin feels clammy. Oh God, this is awful.

'I'll fetch Brother Gavin –'

'No.'

His voice sounds weak. Breathless. It doesn't sound like him at all.

'My lord, you're sick –'

'No.' He opens his eyes again. 'No. Don't ...'

'But what's the *matter*?!'

His head falls forward. He covers his face with his hands. It's appalling: like watching a mountain crumble before your very eyes.

'Oh Pagan ...' Huskily. 'Pagan ...'

'What *is it*?!'

'I don't know what to do.'

His hands. They're quite badly scarred. I've never noticed it before. Lots of little scars – white – like strands of silk. So many scars, for such a young man.

It's funny. He can't be more than – what? Twenty-five? Twenty-six?

Oh hell. What's *happening* here?

'But – what do you mean, my lord?'

No reply. This is hopeless. This can't go on. He has to pull himself together.

'My lord, what's wrong? I don't understand. Is it the Grand Master? Has the Grand Master told you to lay down your arms?'

He looks up.

'*Who told you that?*'

'Is it true? Is that what's happened?'

'No . . .' He shakes his head. 'No, but it will. It will. Brother Felix heard him say . . .'

Whoa. Wait a moment.

'Who's Brother Felix? Is he the knight with Sergeant Tibald?'

'Yes, of course. I can't – you don't – he – I can't –'

'Calm down, my lord.' Seizing his hands, trying to hold them still. 'You don't have to worry. No one in these headquarters is going to take any notice of what Gerard de Ridfort says. You ought to hear them talking about him! They won't obey his orders.'

'No. No, no, that's not – you don't understand. No.'

'Well what, then?'

I can't believe this is happening. He's got to pull himself together. He's *got* to.

'It's finished.' Staring at me. Dazed. 'There's nothing left.'

'What do you mean, there's nothing left?' Christ in a cream cheese sauce. 'Wake up, my lord, wake up. There's still Jerusalem.'

'No. You don't understand. There's nothing left for *me*.'

Gazing at each other, across a vast gulf of misunderstanding. Well I don't know. I mean I really don't know. It's all too deep for yours truly.

Suddenly he sighs, and draws his hands away. They're not shaking any more.

'How can you understand?' he says. 'How many men have you killed? I have killed so many ... I don't even *know* how many. I have been killing men since I was twelve years old. Twelve years old!'

(So?)

'But you're a knight, my lord. I mean, that's what you're here to do. Isn't it?'

'Is it?' He goes grey – quite grey – as if he's about to throw up. 'Then I was born for damnation. For eternal hellfire.'

Oh God. This is insane. I don't know whether to laugh or cry.

'My lord – you're not *serious*.'

'Serious?' Stiffly. 'Of course I'm serious. Jesus said, "Put up thy sword into the sheath". He said, "Turn the other cheek".'

'But that's got nothing to do with *you*.'

'Why not?'

Why not? Why *not*? Because you're perfect. Look at you. Just look at you. If anyone was ever made in God's image it's you, Roland.

'My lord, you must see the difference. You're not an ordinary person. God made you like this. You were made to fight for God.'

'How?'

'Well – um –' (Well I don't know. You tell me. You're the expert.)

'I was born in a land of slaughter, Pagan. I was born on a battlefield. My father is the biggest butcher in Christendom. He took me from the cradle and welded my sword to my hand. And when I was gorged with blood – when my dreams were so full of ghosts that there was no more room for sleep – I went to the monastery of Saint Jerome, and I begged for a place behind its walls. I *begged*. On my *knees*. But the Abbot wouldn't let me in. He said I was born to fight, and I should fight for God, and he sent me to fight for the city of God.'

'Jerusalem.'

'Yes, Jerusalem. I came here to serve the King of Jerusalem. The last king. And I found that the King was a leper. I found that I couldn't even kiss his hand, he smelt so rotten. And I thought: why would God curse the Holy City with a leper king?'

'He wasn't a curse.' Poor old Baldwin. Poor old King Baldwin. 'He was a brave king.'

'But he was a leper, Pagan. A *leper*. It was surely a sign from God. And when I looked around, I saw that his kingdom was as rotten as its king. I saw thieves at every door, monks consorting with women, Christians cheating pilgrims and trading with the Infidel –'

'Well it's no worse than anywhere else!'

'But it ought to be *better*, don't you see? Or what is there here that's worth fighting for?'

It's always the same. The eternal lament of the foreigner. Call this a Holy City? The streets aren't even clean!

'So I appealed to the Church once more, and once more the priests bade me fight. The kingdom couldn't spare me, they said. They told me to join the Templars. To become a Monk of War. They said the Rule of the Order

was perfect in its obedience to the divine will, and that by following the Rule I would become one of God's own liege men.'

'And that's exactly what you *are*!'

He looks up. That look –! Like an enormous weight, settling onto your shoulders.

'The Rule is broken,' he says. 'The Rule is broken by its own guardian. We cannot follow it any more: how can we? It tells us to obey our Grand Master. It tells us to fight to the death. We must break one rule or break another. How can it be our path to salvation now? The path is gone. The truth is gone. There are no rules. There's nothing.'

And he sits there, staring at the floor, with his hands lying open on his knees, the very picture of despair. While I can't even begin to understand what he's saying. It doesn't make sense. So what if the Rule is broken? We'll just make a new Rule. It's not the end of the world.

'My lord, the Rule doesn't matter. What matters is the fight. We still have to fight.'

'For what?'

'For *what*? For our *lives*, that's what!'

'But my life is worthless. It has no meaning in the eyes of God. I have spent it killing and killing . . . for no good cause. The Rule is broken. I have no path. How can I reach salvation if I can't find a path?'

Salvation, salvation. Most of us just take our chances. I don't know, Roland, somehow I can't picture you in hell.

'My lord, I'm not a priest. I have no understanding of these things. If you ask me, I should say that of all the people in the world you're the most likely to go to heaven – but then I'm no expert. All I know . . .' (God, all I know is that

we need you. We *need* you.) 'My lord, without you we're lost. We're all lost, here. Please, my lord, this is my country. You can go home, but where can I go? I have nothing but this. Nothing. And – and you're the only one. There's no one else. If you give up, what will I do? Please, my lord. You're a good man. You can't leave us here. If you leave us, we're finished. *Please . . .*'

God. Did I say that? He's staring – staring – and the blood feels hot in my cheeks. Let go of his arm, Pagan. He looks down as my hand moves: a sleepy, stunned sort of look. Like someone who's just woken up.

Suddenly the door creaks on its hinges. Sergeant Pons peers in.

He sees Roland, and gapes.

'My lord! Are you all right?'

'What?' Blinking. 'Yes. Yes, I'm all right.'

'But what are you doing down there?'

'Nothing.' Roland heaves himself upright. Climbs to his feet. 'Nothing. What is it?'

'My lord, I've been looking all over. We need to call a council. We need to make decisions –'

'Yes, of course.' Glancing at me. He looks pale, still, but collected. Amazing how fast he can recover when he wants to. 'We'll call a general chapter, to break the news. Then I want to discuss our strategy with you and Brother Felix, sergeant. Brother Felix will be very useful with his first-hand knowledge. It will help us to know what we're up against. Pagan?'

'My lord?'

He seems about to speak, but acts instead. Laying a hand on my shoulder. His grip is as firm as a rock: not heavy,

just strong. He stands there, looking down at me, with the colour coming back to his face.

'Thank you,' he says at last. 'Thank you, Pagan. You are right, of course.'

And he smiles before leaving the room.

124

Part Three
September, 1187

The city of Jerusalem stands alone against Saladin's
army of Infidels.

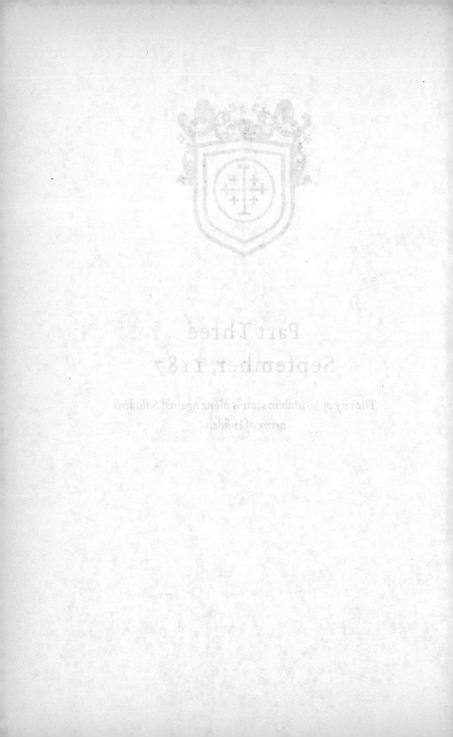

Part Three
September 1187

The city of Jerusalem stands alone against Saladin's army of infidels.

Chapter 7

From Tancred's Tower, you can see their flags quite clearly – flashes of colour in the fitful gusts of wind. A hot, dry wind. Kicking up dust in their faces. Carrying snatches of sound across the city walls: the babble of voices, the clash of iron, the whinnying of horses and mules.

Very quiet, on this side. Everyone's watching. Like birds in a nest, watching a cat at the base of the tree.

Except that there are hundreds of cats ... maybe thousands. All properly trained and able-bodied. While on this side, at least fifty women and children for every man.

'There.' Roland points. 'Look there.' A tent rises, billowing, over the busy, steel-capped heads. White and blue and silver. A real home from home.

Must be Saladin's.

'What is it?' Balian, squinting. Who would have thought that the great Lord Balian – Balian 'just call me Chivalry' of Ibelin – would turn out to be short-sighted? Quite small, too. And getting on in years. A solid, serious man, balding on top, with a little mouth and a big neck. Quite a shock, after all those stories.

Not the kind of looks to inspire confidence. Not like Roland's. Still – give Balian his due. He did repel Saladin's attack on Tyre. And he didn't do that by posing heroically against a majestic mountainous backdrop.

'It's a tent, my lord.' (Roland.) 'Very fine. Would it be the Sultan's?'

'Without a doubt.'

And what are those things, over there? Like cages on wheels. Cages or scaffolding. Don't like the look of them at all.

'My lord?'

'Yes, Pagan.'

'Those strange wooden structures ...'

'They are mangonels.'

Mangonels! I've heard about mangonels. A mangonel can throw a rock as big as a donkey. And Saladin's got *three* of them!

Balian is frowning. 'We must strengthen this tower with sacks full of cotton and hay. This tower and the citadel.'

'I've already given the order, my lord.' Roland's motto: be prepared. He's not stupid. He's got every woman, child and greybeard in Jerusalem sewing ox and camel hides into covers for the city's exposed woodwork, so that it's protected against the terrible Greek fire. He's put buckets of sand all

along the top of the city walls. He's removed the awnings from across the streets because they're a fire hazard, and posted watches and rationed water and built up great piles of wood and dung, so that fires can be lit and lead melted at short notice.

He's done everything the Patriarch would let him do. And now Balian's come along and done the rest. Raided the treasury, distributed arms, even stripped the silver from the roof of the Holy Sepulchre.

Just shows where a bit of political clout can get you.

'We've one advantage, anyway,' Balian mutters. The sun will be in his eyes of a morning.'

'Not only that, my lord. The pool of Siloam is his only water supply, and it's right under the southern wall.' Roland doesn't take his eyes from the enemy camp as he speaks. 'A couple of archers or a mangonel stationed near the gate and we'll have it completely covered.'

'That's true.'

'The only other spring is two parasangs away. We could even send out a company – ambush the path –'

Balian grunts. Thank God he's arrived, is all I can say. With Balian and Roland in command we might actually pull through this awful predicament. Standing there together, squinting into the wind, solid and strong and well-armoured – they're our only hope.

'He's brought a team of sappers with him,' says Balian. 'That much I do know, though I haven't seen them in action.'

'His cavalry hasn't fared well,' says Roland. 'Not that his horses have ever been worth boasting about. I believe his engineering support is what really gives him the edge.'

'Byzantine, most of them.'

'Truly?'

'Never trust a Greek.'

Suddenly a detachment peels off Saladin's main formation. Three riders, one carrying a flag. All of them heading straight for us.

'My lord –'

'Yes, I see. Sergeant Gildoin! I want women and children off these walls! Understand? All non-combatants!'

'Yes, my lord!'

He'll be lucky. The only way to keep children out from under your feet on occasions like this is to feed them to the nearest wild animal. And what I want to know is, why send them away at all? Why not use them? When I was that age, I had the eyes of an eagle. My aim was so good, I could have knocked out Saladin's two front teeth from halfway across the kingdom.

Give that pair of urchins a few slings and stones and they'll probably annihilate the whole Infidel army before the sun goes down.

'Brother Felix! Archers in position, please!'

'Yes, Brother!'

'And I want a full complement ready on the rock piles.'

'Yes, Brother, and what about the fires? Shall we light the fires?'

'Not yet. I'll give the word.'

'Yes, Brother.'

That Lord Felix is fast on his feet. Shoots off like an arrow. Suddenly people are moving again: dashing about, waving their arms, gathering up their axes and helmets and

dazed platoons. If I was a Templar sergeant, I'd have a platoon by now. When your troops are mostly merchants, potters, shepherds, tanners, barbers, tax collectors, cobblers, carpenters, farriers, smiths, apothecaries, cooks, thieves, notaries and bath-house attendants, you have to divide them into nice, small groups and put an experienced Templar at the head of each one. That's why poor old Bonetus has that line of overweight shopkeepers trailing after him like a flock of ducklings.

Thank heavens I'm just a lowly squire.

'Pagan.'

'Yes, my lord?'

'You have good eyes. Lord Balian wants to know, are any of those approaching heralds wearing a red turban?'

'Yes, my lord. Just the one.'

Balian nods. 'Malik al-Adil,' he says, and Roland raises an eyebrow.

'The Sultan's brother?'

'In person.'

Saladin's brother! Riding a sleek bay palfrey, fully armoured, crimson shield, can't see his face yet. What a temptation. One small arrow . . .

Balian steps forward, clinking in his chain mail. It looks battered and dirty, almost black in places. His squire can't have cleaned it in months. Funny sort of squire. Seems to spend all his time propping up Balian's standard. Nice job, if you can get it: a walking flag pole. Probably too old to do anything else (judging from the grey hair). Never seen a squire with grey hair before.

Saladin's brother has no beard. He reins in beneath the tower, craning his neck to look up at Balian. Framed in an

embrasure, Balian leans out over the sheer drop of the wall, his standard flapping above his head. Their eyes meet.

'Balian Lord of Ibelin!'

'Malik Saif ed-Din al-Adil.'

'Behold the forces of Yusuf Salah ed-Din, my master.' Malik flings out his arm, dramatically. 'Yusuf Salah ed-Din desires no bloodshed in this most holy place. Surrender the city now and he will guarantee the lives of all its inhabitants.'

'We shall not surrender this holy city.'

'Yusuf Salah ed-Din urges you to consider your weak position. Your king is our captive. Your forces are few. Resist us now and we will butcher every man, woman and child behind those walls. Submit now and we shall be merciful in the sight of God.'

'In the sight of God, there can only be one outcome. We shall not surrender this holy city.'

'So be it.'

And there goes our last chance. Wheeling his horse about and kicking it into a canter. Little clouds of dust rising at every hoofbeat.

The silence up here is as thick as beaten cream.

'That man has fourteen wives, so I've heard,' Balian suddenly remarks. He glances at Roland, and cracks a brittle smile. 'No wonder he spends all his time in the field.'

A shaky sort of laugh ripples across the roof of the tower. Roland, of course, simply fails to respond. He doesn't approve of jokes like that. Instead he turns to me.

'Go and tell Brother Felix I want axemen standing by all along the north wall. Every ten paces. Then report back here. Understand?'

'Yes, my lord.'

'Repeat it.'

'Axemen standing by along the north wall. Every ten paces.'

'Get going.'

And so it begins.

Who-o-om-CRASH!

God preserve us. That was close. Where did it land? The splinters of rock still pattering down from the sky.

'Pagan!'

Roland up ahead – he hardly faltered. Beckoning. Get a move on! White tunic, red cross – in that outfit he's a moving target.

Scurrying behind him, bent double. Through the chains of labouring men who pass great slabs of limestone from hand to hand. A steady flow of ammunition to the defenders at the wall. I don't envy our opponents. Imagine climbing a ladder with huge chunks of pavement falling past your ears! Not to mention the showers of boiling lead.

You wouldn't get me volunteering, that's for sure.

Who-o-om-CRASH!

Ouch. Chip of rock. Just a scratch. Hardly any blood at all.

One of the merlons, knocked right down – a solid chunk of masonry two strides long and half a stride thick. Leaving a great big hole between the embrasures.

'Cover that gap!' (Roland.) 'You! You and you! Get over there!'

Someone howling. Look back – God – a bloody stump – dangling . . .

The missile's taken his arm off.

Don't look. Don't look and you won't be sick.

'You! In the arming cap! Take that man to the surgeon's station!' Roland's voice is hoarse and hard. 'Sergeant! Eyes front! Look out!'

Sure enough, it's another ladder. Wobbling wood, scraping against the stone. Roland leaps to the embrasure and kicks at one of the cross-rungs. It swings back, falters, then slams onto the wall again. Someone down there knows how to hold a ladder.

'Over here! Push! Pagan, push!'

You can feel the vibrations of their feet through the shafts. One – two – three – *push*! What a weight. One – two – three – *push*! Useless. Some idiot throws a fire-stick right past my head. Whoosh! Somersaulting down . . . down . . . misses the first climber. Singes the second one's hair. Whoosh! Another, leaving a trail of sparks and smoke.

'Out of the way, damn you!'

Pulled back and elbowed aside. Make room for the boulder, please! A six-man stone, balanced on the very edge . . . four wooden levers inserted underneath . . . and all together *push*!

Down it goes. Piercing screams as the earth shakes. Looks as though we've broken the ladder –

'Pagan.'

And on we go. There's Sergeant Maynard, plastered with soot, drinking water from a pail. Past the next ladder, and the boiling crowd around it. Axes swinging. Stones flying. People screaming with excitement.

Who-o-om-CRASH!

'Sergeant! Sergeant Tibald!' Roland's voice cuts across the confusion. Rockhead! Didn't recognise him. Dripping with sweat, powdered with dust and ashes, naked from the waist up. He turns, breathing heavily.

'Spread the cover, sergeant! We need more men to the west!'

'Yes, my lord.' (Coughing.) 'You! Aimery! Get down there and watch that gate! You too – and you! That's right.'

'I don't like the way they're bunching these missiles.' Roland squints into the sun. 'It looks as though they're trying to clear particular spaces . . .'

An arrow shatters on the ground not two steps away from his right foot. He glances down without really seeing. Rockhead lets out a hiss.

'How many ladders, my lord? Do you know?'

'Sixteen. At the last count.'

'Saladin must have cleared all the forests in Samaria.'

Sudden uproar from the nearest knot of defenders. Spin around and God! An Infidel! Bright blood – open mouth – flashing sword – screaming and screaming . . .

He disappears in a thrashing tangle of bodies. Hasn't a hope. Hasn't a hope. But there's another one. Rising over the heads – look out!

'*Look out!*'

A blade jabs out of that boiling mess. Straight to the Infidel's stomach. He drops like a stone . . . reeling back into empty air . . . disappearing. But the next one takes his place.

Who-o-om-CRASH!

God! So close!

Rockhead falls.

'Sergeant!'

He's still alive. Clutching his right arm ... right shoulder. Torn skin on his chest. Doesn't *look* too bad. Face screwed up. Eyes shut. Gasping for breath.

'Sergeant?'

Bit of rock must have got him. A big bit. Cracked ribs, maybe?

'*My lord!*'

Where is he? God. I should be with him. There he is. Defending the wall. (Don't tell me they've broken through *there!*) Legs planted firmly apart, both hands on his sword hilt, chopping and chopping and chopping at the ladder-load of Infidels below ...

Leaps backward, away from a swinging mace. (Last gasp assault from a dying Turk.) Nearly falls flat on his back, but recovers just in time. Someone in quilted buckram comes to his rescue, surging forward with a raised spear. Ploughing into the very next Infidel.

Rockhead moans. Got to do something ...

'*My lord!*'

Roland hears me. Turns and looks, bent double, holding his side.

God – the old wound. Don't tell me it's playing up again. He moves over quickly, still stooped, with his hand still pressed to his midriff.

The skirt of his tunic is stained dark red.

'My lord, should I take him ...?'

'What is it? Bones?'

'The ribs, I think. Collarbone, maybe. My lord –'

'Yes, all right.' Breathing raggedly. 'All right, take him – no. Wait. No, you might not find me again. Let me just see if there's anyone –'

WHOMP!

Overhead, that terrible sound. And a wave of flame washing across the top of the wall . . .

'Greek fire! Greek fire!'

Burning puddles.

'Greek fire!'

'Sand! Sand! You and you!'

'*Where are the ox-hides?*'

I don't believe this. I don't believe this. Lord, I cry unto thee; make haste unto me; give ear unto my voice when I cry unto thee.

People beating at the flames with cured skins. People pounding past from all directions. Running. Yelling.

'*Man your posts!*' (Roland.) 'Get back there! Back! Get back there! You – *watch that ladder!*'

'Oh my lord. My lord, your wound. You're hurt . . .'

He looks down at me. Blue eyes big and bloodshot in a grimy face. Suddenly very still.

'Stop crying, Pagan.'

What?

'There's nothing to cry about.' (Gently.) 'Not yet.'

But I'm not crying! Am I? Reach up . . . and there they are. The tears. Christ in a cream cheese sauce.

Cheers from way down the wall somewhere. Theirs or ours? Roland cranes his neck to see. The smell is awful – sulphur? Charcoal? Whatever it is, it's the stuff they use to make Greek fire. You can hardly see for the smoke.

Rockhead starts coughing.

'Leave me ... I'll manage,' he squawks. (Every word sounds as if he's being stabbed.) 'It's nothing ... I can tell ...'

'*You there! With the shield!*' Roland raises his voice. 'Yes, you! Come and take this man to the surgeon's station!'

'No ... my lord ... you'll deplete ... our defence ...'

'Don't concern yourself, sergeant. The enemy is withdrawing, at least for the present.'

They are? Through the drifts of smoke you can just see Lord Felix. He's making the sign of retreat. Behind him, a ragged collection of armoured shopkeepers are making other signs, rude ones, in the general direction of Saladin.

'Praise God, my lord!'

'Hmmmm.' Roland scans the wall, up and down. There's a noticeable lack of movement. Everyone seems to be waiting ... waiting ... A charred rock here, a smashed bow there, a person spreading sand, a crumpled body, an empty bucket, a trampled cloak, a nasty smell, a pool of blood.

Roland looks up at the blushing sky.

'It's getting late,' he says – and moves off quickly, to assess the situation.

'Wake up, Pagan.'

What – what the ...?

'Come on. Up.'

But I only just went to sleep!

'Go 'way.'

'It's an emergency, Pagan. They've broken through the wall. Now get up. Hurry.'

They've what? What have they done? It's not even daylight! Roland half dressed, groping for his boots. A pale, pinkish light filtering through the window. Somebody hovering near the door.

'Go,' says Roland. 'Tell Lord Balian I'm on my way.'

The figure disappears. Outside, the scuffle of hurrying feet. Low, urgent voices on the stairwell. A distant sound of clashing iron.

'My lord? What's happened?'

'What do you think?' He pulls on one boot, then another. 'Their sappers have been mining the wall. They've made a breach, at last.'

'Where?'

'Near the Gate of the Column.'

God preserve us. Where's my swordbelt? Feeling around in the gloom.

'Hurry *up*, Pagan.'

I'm hurrying, I'm hurrying!

'How big is the breach, my lord?'

'I don't know, I haven't seen it yet. Move!'

Just as well I'm dressed. Didn't even take my boots off. Must have passed out the moment I crossed the threshold, too tired to do anything but hit the ground.

And pretty hard ground it is, too. This room wasn't made for sleeping. What is it – some kind of storeroom? Seems to be piled high with bits of old furniture. Funny place to pick for a doze.

'Hurry up, Pagan!'

'I'm ready, my lord. Here I am.'

And off we rush. It's quite a distance, from Tancred's Tower to the Gate of the Column. Down the stairs (two

flights), out the door, under an arch, turn left, squeeze through an alley, up five steps, down nine, past a cistern, over a roof, slip in a puddle, and you're halfway there. People sleeping in corners. A dead dog on a pile of fetid garbage. A soldier from the city garrison – I know the face, forget the name. Lots of fuzzy black hair and a big, hooked nose in the torchlight. 'They've broken through! They've broken through!' Dashing past to rouse the city.

'My lord?'

'What?'

'Not that way, my lord. That's a dead end.'

Other people, heading in the same direction. Yelling as they run. A little knot of women, huddled round a fire in a murky alcove, crying out, alarmed. Somebody pounding up behind us.

'My lord!'

Sergeant Gildoin, gasping for breath. Still pulling on his armour, bleary-eyed.

'Hurry, sergeant. They've made a breach.'

You can hear it quite plainly now: the screaming, thundering, crashing, scraping, roaring sound of battle. The sound that goes through your heart like a knife. Can't be much further. Only one more block to the Gate of the Column.

'You! You there!' Roland grabs at a scurrying figure with a bandaged head. 'Where is Lord Balian?'

'Who? What?'

'Lord Balian! Where is he?'

No help from *that* quarter. Poor fellow's lost his wits. Stands and stares like a dumb animal.

Roland throws him aside impatiently.

'My lord!'

Pons. Where did he come from?

'This way, my lord! This way!'

He dives up the covered stairs from which he emerged, and Roland follows, drawing his sword. Here we go! The air's thick with dust. The stairs are strewn with rubble. The noise is deafening.

'Watch out! Watch yourself!'

'Over here!'

'They're coming!'

It's all so confused. A mass of broken stone; flaring torches; struggling people. Floor tiles – was a house knocked over? The loose debris underfoot, sliding away at each step. A wedge of tightly packed bodies. Hundreds of them, and all ours. All ours! All ours, all armed, all ready for action.

'Oof!'

Watch where you're going, dunghead! I'm on *your* side.

'Pagan.'

Look around. Where is Roland? Ah! Over near that tallish building . . . three storeys . . . with Balian on the roof. I suppose it's what you'd call a 'strategic standpoint'. Clear view of the chaos.

Sudden roar. Whip round. The wedge of troops, breaking up. Can't see – God help us – are they pushing through? A shower of arrows, some distance away. Archers. Stationed on the walls either side of the breach. Smart move, that. Balian's? Doesn't seem to be stopping the enemy.

I need to empty my bladder.

'Pagan . . .'

It's Arnulf, stumbling out of the smoky haze. Staring. Falling. Arnulf?

'Arn?'

Someone behind him.

'*Yaaoooaah!*'

Turk! Turk! Help! Sword! Duck!

'*Yaah! Yaah!*'

Battleaxe – heavy. Swing and miss. Now! *Now!* Under the armpit!

Got him!

No. Just the arm. Watch that foot!

'Oof!'

Hard kick. Fall on stone, hit my arm. God, my arm. God, the axe! *Roll over!*

CHUNK!

His blade, buried in the rubble. Just missed my shoulder. He pulls it out, swings it over his head, staggering under the weight. His legs! Go for his legs!

Straight to the knees. *Down* he goes. Axe spins away – watch his hands – boot in the chest. Ouch. Ouch. My ribs. My ribs. Can't breathe . . .

Thrown on my back. His weight on top. *Knife! He's got a knife!*

'Haah!'

Roland.

A warm gush of blood. Infidel blood. The weight falls away. Rolling away, heavily, the arm flopping down. The knife chinking on stone.

The blood . . .

Dragged upright. Collapsing again on fluffy cotton knees. Roland's arm like an iron bar against my shoulder. His urgent, gasping voice.

'What is it? Where is it? Show me!'

Shaking my head.

'*Show me!*'

'It's nothing.' Miracle! My breath's come back again. 'It's just a kick. In the chest. That's all.'

'What's *this*, then?'

Look down. He's holding my arm, and there's a nasty gash across the elbow. How on earth did that happen? Didn't feel a thing.

'I don't know, I don't know what it is . . .'

'*Then I'll tell you what it is! It's what happens when you don't obey orders!*' He's practically shouting – I've never seen him so angry. 'Next time, when I want you to come, you'll *come!* Understand?'

'Yes, my lord.'

'Instead of stopping and gawking like a silly damned sheep in a slaughterhouse!'

'I'm sorry, my lord.'

'I've already lost two squires to these blood-glutted savages! Do you think I want to lose *you*, as well?'

'My lord!'

I know that voice. The Master-Sergeant, standing there dissolving in his own sweat.

'Lord Balian wants to bring in a mounted squadron,' he pants. 'Lord Balian wants Templar horses . . . you in charge . . . right now . . .'

'I'm coming.' Roland nudges me forward. 'Take my squire to the surgeon's station and I'll come at once.'

'But –'

'No! My lord! I'm perfectly all right!'

'I want his arm properly dressed. Tell Brother Gavin to check for fractures or broken bones.'

'Yes, my lord.'

God preserve us! I can't go with Garlic-Breath! He'll hang my gizzards out to dry!

'Wait – please – I'm not –'

'Be quiet, Pagan. As for you, sergeant, you listen to me.' (Roland places the tip of his finger gently on the Master-Sergeant's labouring ribcage.) 'I know all about you and your affairs. And if the slightest harm comes to this boy while he's out of my sight, you probably won't live long enough to regret it. Understand?'

He understands, all right. You can tell by the way his eyes slink around like hunted animals.

'Yes, my lord.'

'Good.'

It's daylight, at last. As we stumble away from the breach, a cock crows somewhere deep inside the city. I can hear it even through the roar of a thousand hysterical fighters.

That bird's got guts.

Chapter 8

What a bizarre situation.

I mean, the *room* for a start. So rich and gaudy. The silk pillows! The carved shutters! The little ebony tables, inlaid with ivory and mother-of-pearl, too small to support anything but a scent bottle. At least a dozen of the fussy things, scattered across a peacock-coloured Persian rug. I mean, what are they *for*?

Jade lamps, too. Gold-embroidered tapestries. Chairs like thrones and doors like the gates of heaven. The Patriarch's taste for luxury would leave King Solomon's for dead. And in the midst of all this splendour, the dilapidated human beings. Lord Felix, pale as sea salt, a four-day growth on his chin. The Master-Sergeant, stained and creased like a bundle of dirty laundry left out in a dust storm. Lord Roland, heavy-eyed, still wearing the same old blood-spattered tunic

(now more brown than white). Brother Gavin, in a stupor of fatigue.

Only the Patriarch belongs in this room, and even he's not looking his best. His face is thinner; his colour is sickly; his fingernails have been bitten down so far that he's drawn blood. Hasn't left him much to scratch with.

'These fleas,' he says at last, breaking the awful silence. 'They seem to be reaching plague proportions.'

The Master-Sergeant grunts. No one else says anything. We just scratch ourselves, thoughtfully.

'I've tried pepper,' the Lily continues, 'but it doesn't seem to work. Is there anything more I can do?'

'You can try burning hay.' (Lord Felix.) 'That helps with mosquitoes.'

'It doesn't help with fleas. I've tried,' says the Master-Sergeant.

Another pause, but you can't stop the Lily.

'I've heard that if you wear a little piece of fur close to your skin, then all the fleas will congregate on that –'

'Wormwood,' says Gavin, suddenly. Thought he was asleep. His eyes are glazed, and he speaks in a monotone. 'Wormwood or tansy or winter savory. Or rue. A few drops of wormwood tea. A scattering of tansy leaves. Or you can steep some horehound in milk, and use that. Even an infusion of elder will do the trick. Herbs are very effective repellents.'

In that case, perhaps we ought to try some on Saladin. Since nothing else seems to work. Ho hum. Where is Lord Balian?

'My apologies, everyone.' Lo and behold! He walks

through the door. 'I was detained by new tidings. Is everyone here?'

'Yes, my lord.' A weary chorus.

'Good. Then we can begin.' He throws himself onto one of the Lily's luxurious seats – and I don't like the way he does it. I don't like the way his foot taps the floor. I don't like the strain in his muscles. 'Lord Roland? We'll start with your assessment, I think.'

'Yes, my lord.' Roland clears his throat. 'My lord, the breach has doubled its size in the last day. Our defences are stretched to the limits. Already the south and south-west walls are dangerously undermanned.'

'And how much longer can we hold out? In your estimation.'

All eyes on Roland, who drops his gaze to the floor.

'I believe – no more than three days, at the most.'

(You what? You didn't tell me that! You said we were strong in our endurance! You *said*!)

Around the room, protesting voices.

'If you please.' Balian raises a hand. 'I had reached practically the same conclusion myself. Brother, do you have the casualty figures?'

Gavin blinks. He looks very old, all of a sudden.

'Seven hundred and thirteen dead, my lord. Sixteen hundred and sixty-five wounded.'

God preserve us.

Roland crosses himself.

'And you, Master-Sergeant?' (Balian.) 'What are your figures?'

'I don't know about exact figures, my lord.' The Master-Sergeant scratches himself absent-mindedly. It's hard to

judge what some people might have hoarded away in their cupboards. But I'd estimate there are supplies for a week – perhaps ten days. No more.'

'Thank you.'

A long, long silence. Feel as if I'm going to be sick. As if I'm going to vomit all over the Lily's fancy carpet. Swallowing hard, again and again.

'There's something else I've just been told,' Balian announces. 'Fortunately, there is at least one Orthodox Greek in this city who holds Christianity dearer than the works of the devil. He has passed on the information that Saladin's personal adviser is an Orthodox scholar from Jerusalem by the name of Joseph Batit. Somehow – don't ask me how – Joseph Batit has made contact with the Orthodox community within these walls.'

He stops for a moment. The look on his face – you'd think there was a bad taste in his mouth.

'The Orthodox community,' he says at last, like some-one spitting out a bitter poison, 'has promised to open the gates to Saladin as soon as the opportunity presents itself.'

'What?'

I can't believe it. I can't *believe* it. The Patriarch leaps to his feet. Jaws drop – everyone's.

'But I don't understand.' Gavin, bewildered. 'Why would they want to do that?'

'Because they're foul, satanic, hypocritical heretics, that's why!' The Lily's gone red. Quite red. 'We must kill them all! Now! Every last filthy one of them!'

'Somehow I don't think that's going to solve our problem,' says Balian, in a dry sort of voice. 'Though I agree they deserve it.'

'Then what are we going to do?'

There must be an answer. Look to Roland. He has his eyes on the floor again, sitting there like some kind of long-nosed, stone-faced statue. No matter how hard I stare, I can't get him to raise his head.

'I believe there's only one thing we can do.' Balian speaks very quietly. 'I believe –'

'– that we should make a last great sortie and give our lives to God as the Lord Jesus sacrificed his life for us!'

Felix. Hasn't said a word until now. His white face gleams with sweat and devotion.

Probably a little mad from lack of sleep.

'That *is* one possibility.' Balian doesn't sound too enthusiastic. Thank God. 'I know there are several people who support the idea . . .'

'But this is insane!' The shrill, frantic voice of the Patriarch. 'This is no more than suicide!'

Felix shakes his head. 'Not suicide, Father. Martyrdom.' You can see that the notion really appeals to him. You can also see that it doesn't appeal to the Lily. He's practically climbing the wall.

'*Martyrdom!*' he screeches. (No one's going to make a martyr out of *him*!) Suddenly he pulls himself together; takes a deep breath; wipes the palms of his hands on his fine silk gown. 'Certainly it would be martyrdom,' he quavers. 'But it would be martyrdom also for our women and children. With their men gone, they will face inevitable slavery. I will not give my blessing to so impious an action. Is it right that we should abandon our helpless dependants?'

No, it's not. It's not right at all. Come on, everyone. Let's be realistic. Let's live to fight another day.

'I agree with Patriarch Heraclius.' (Hooray! Balian agrees!) 'It's folly to waste more lives defending the indefensible. As things stand now, we have a good chance of negotiating reasonable terms of surrender. The weaker we become, the less chance we'll have of making any gains. Is that not so, Lord Roland?'

Everyone looks from one lord to the other – and Roland raises his eyes, at last. Impossible to read his expression.

'Yes,' he says. 'It is so.'

'Then I shall act on this advice, and seek terms from Saladin.'

There it is. What we've all been waiting for. What we've all been dreading. Don't know whether to rejoice or despair. Don't know what I feel.

Gavin falls back in his seat with a long and weary sigh.

'I shall go at once,' Balian continues. There's a new energy in his voice: fresh colour in his cheeks. Not surprising, really. He has a wife and son, after all. 'I shall call for a parley on his own ground. We can both go, Lord Roland, if you do not object.'

Roland says nothing. He simply nods in agreement. Balian glances at Felix, whose eyes are big and dark and full of tears. 'I must ask you to stay, Lord Felix, to command the city's defence in our absence.'

'You don't think I would go?' Felix spits it out, wildly. 'I would *never* go! *Never!*'

'Don't worry, my lord, you won't have to. I am the one who will be remembered until the end of time as the man who gave Jerusalem to the heathens.' Balian sounds quite calm, but his face is too painful to look at.

So that's the great Saladin.

Bit of a shock, really. Would have missed him in a crowd. Slight build, sad face, big nose, medium height, conservative taste in clothing. No bloodstained teeth, bat's wings, devil's horns or anything else diabolic. Just a normal-looking human being.

Which is more than you can say for some of the other Infidels squeezed into this tent. That ghastly wreck over there, for example: the one with the face that's just a ball of scar tissue, with a single eye embedded in the shiny red ridges. Or that hulking, hairy monster glowering across the top of Saladin's head. What a collection. All bathed in blue – the blue of the tent walls – as the sun beats down through the fabric and turns this portable palace into an oven.

Flies buzzing from mouth to mouth. Hands flapping. Armour clinking. Outside, the muffled noise of battle.

Inside, an embarrassing pause. Balian's introduced himself. Saladin's introduced himself. Now what?

Now Balian introduces his second in command.

'This is Lord Roland Roucy de Bram of the Templar knights.'

The temperature seems to fall a notch. You can feel their hackles rising.

Saladin turns a cold, bleak eye on Roland and his distinctive white tunic with its blood-red cross.

'I have entertained your Grand Master many times in this tent, Lord Roland,' he remarks – with that flowery and precise courtesy that everyone's always talking about. You've got to admit he's damned fluent. His accent may be thick,

but his vocabulary's amazing. 'Your Grand Master is the only Templar knight besides yourself who has ever been granted this privilege.' Meaning that every other Templar knight has been slaughtered on the threshold. It's no secret that Saladin doesn't like Templars.

Feeling's mutual, of course.

'Now, my lord Balian.' The Great Man gets down to business. 'You have come on a mission of peace, I understand.'

Balian nods.

'We have come to discuss an end to the fighting, my lord.'

'Good, I am thankful. There has been too much bloodshed on this holy ground.' A sigh, a nod, a pious gesture. 'Do you wish, then, to lay down your arms?'

'Only upon certain conditions.'

'Ah.'

Loads of meaning in a little word. It's obvious the Great Man's not about to give in easily. It's obvious from the bland sort of way he raises his eyebrows.

'But my lord Balian, I fear you have nothing left with which to bargain.' (Gently.) 'My standard has just been raised on the city wall, as you know.'

'The city has not yet fallen.'

'It is only a matter of time.'

Balian takes a deep breath. He's sweating buckets, but otherwise he seems composed. It probably helps when you've got a face like something hacked out of hardwood.

'If Jerusalem falls, it will be at a most terrible cost,' he says. 'A negotiated surrender will prevent that.'

'Perhaps it will. Unfortunately, I swore an oath many

years ago that I would take Jerusalem by sword. Only your *unconditional* surrender will absolve me from my oath.'

Christ in a cream cheese sauce. Balian swallows. Saladin waits. Look to Lord Roland. He hasn't taken his eyes off the Great Man since making his entrance. Hasn't twitched a muscle, either. Impossible to tell what he thinks.

'An unconditional surrender is out of the question.' Balian finds his voice at last. It sounds strained. 'You must realise that no one in the city will accept this alternative. You must *see* that.'

'I'm sorry.' (Saladin.) 'It is a matter of honour.'

'Is honour more important than innocent lives?'

Roland speaks out. Quite calmly, but with that familiar hint of disdain. (As in, 'Pagan, is that apple core there for a purpose?' or 'Pagan, did you say you were finished cleaning this shield?'.) Saladin turns his head, slowly. Such a wealth of menace in such a trivial movement.

'You come from across the sea, Lord Roland, do you not?'

'I was born in the Frankish lands, yes.'

'Then you are probably not acquainted with the history of this kingdom. If you were, you would appreciate the irony of your remark. When you talk of innocent lives, Lord Roland, you make me think of the lives lost ninety years ago, when your forefathers took Jerusalem from mine. Clearly you are not aware that the only inhabitants to escape from the city with their lives on that occasion were the Governor Iftikhar ad-Daula and his bodyguard. Every other man, woman and child was slain by the Christian soldiers. I have heard that the mosque of al-Aqsa, which you now call your Temple, was knee-deep in our dead.'

He stops for a moment, and his dark face grows darker – as dark as a storm-cloud. Let's just hope the storm doesn't break. Yes? No? Roland says nothing – and it's probably the right thing to do. At least it allows Saladin to take a few deep breaths and calm down.

'It is not my wish to descend to the level of this Christian barbarity,' he murmurs. 'However, such wounds leave very deep scars.'

Sudden noise in the distance. Hard to tell – a muffled roar. Voices, perhaps? Thousands and thousands of swelling voices . . .

Rush for the exit. Balian first, as fast as a flea. Then a tight knot of Infidels. Scraping past their armoured huddle, through a press of perfumed silk. Wriggling free, and – there!

Balian turns. He grabs my arm.

'What's happening? Tell me! I can't see!'

You get a pretty good view from the Mount of Olives. The entire west wall, with the Golden Gate, and the Temple behind it . . . the Gate of Josophat, the spire of St Anne's . . . up along the north wall a bit, and smoke rising against the sky. A real mess, on the north wall.

'Your standard is down, Lord Saladin.' Roland's voice, behind me. 'Your standard is down, and your men are driven back. See for yourself. The city has not fallen.'

A burst of chatter from the Infidels. Balian's face, as bright as silver. Roland, shading his eyes. And Saladin, strolling up with his retinue. Doesn't seem especially concerned.

'You have gained a little time. Nothing more,' he says. 'It is a temporary setback. We shall regroup.'

'You may regroup, Lord Saladin, but my men will fight to the death!' Balian, transformed. The hot blood flaming in his cheeks and eyes and nostrils. 'They will fight to the death, and they will take everything with them! Their prisoners! Their possessions! And *everything in the city that you hold sacred!*'

Aha. That's got him. That's really got him. Look at his hands.

'But your own holy places –'

'Our own holy places. Everything.'

Long pause. Absolute stillness. All eyes on Saladin, watching his shuttered face. Hardly daring to breathe, as he stands there looking at the ground. Thinking. Deciding.

Suddenly he lifts his head.

'In truth, it comes as no surprise,' he announces. 'Unbelievers have little reverence. They treat their sacred things like dog's dung.' His voice is very brisk. Detached. His expression is calm. 'So be it. I shall free every citizen upon your surrender, Lord Balian, at a ransom of ten dinars for every man, five for every woman, and one for every child.'

Hooray!

'Ten dinars?' Balian scratches his chest. 'What about our paupers? There must be twenty thousand of them ...'

'And a lump sum for the paupers. Say ... one hundred thousand.'

'*One hundred thousand dinars?*' Balian nearly chokes on his own tongue.

'Five dinars each. A fair price, I think.'

'For a bunch of diseased cripples?' (Balian.) 'You ought to be paying *us* for taking them off your hands!'

Roland coughs, in a meaningful sort of way. And it makes Saladin smile.

'Very well.' The Great Man concedes a point. 'Seventy thousand.'

Balian shakes his head.

'We can't make seventy. Twenty.'

'Twenty!' The smile grows broader. 'I could get more than that for twenty thousand blind lepers in the slave markets of Baghdad.' 'Twenty for ten, then. Twenty thousand for ten thousand.'

'Fifty for ten.'

'Thirty.'

'Thirty for five.'

'Seven.'

'Done.'

Amazing. Just amazing. I can hardly believe my ears. Is this how kingdoms rise and fall? It sounds like haggling in a fish market.

Glance at Roland, who catches my eye.

'So we are agreed, then.' (Saladin.) 'Thirty thousand dinars for seven thousand paupers, and for the rest –'

'Ten, five and one, I know,' says Balian.

'And fifty dinars for each knight.'

'*Fifty?*'

'At least.' Saladin sounds surprised. 'Surely, Lord Balian, for a man of your stature? You must be worth ten times as much.'

What a gall. What a cheek. What a sly devil. You can see the glint in his sidelong glance.

That Saladin's no fool.

'All right, fifty.' Balian succumbs, scowling. 'Fifty dinars.'

'Good. Then that's settled.' The Great Man gazes out over Jerusalem. Over the Temple Mount, the sheer white walls, the golden dome, the roofs, the towers, the pillars of smoke, the gates, the markets, the churches, the palaces, the Holy Sepulchre. Master of all he surveys.

Historic moment.

'The siege is lifted,' he says.

They've found their way to Templar headquarters. Hundreds of them, all soiled, all starving, all desperate. Clustered around the northern entrance, in the shadow of the golden dome. Welf, poor sod, is on guard duty. He looks like a hen that's hatched a brood of giant locusts who are busy eating everything in sight.

We're hardly within hailing distance when a shuffling hunchback emerges from the interior, and triggers a push for the door.

'All right! Get back! Back, I said!' Welf bars the way with his staff. 'You. Yes you.' (Jerking his head.) 'You next.'

A wail of protest, as someone small and skinny slips beneath his arm. Over the pleading, outstretched hands Welf catches sight of Roland, and his big face lights up.

Shall we risk it, or will they tear us to pieces?

'God have mercy on us all.' Roland, beside me. Stopping in his tracks to watch the hunchback scurry by. A pathetic, greyish old creature, his ransom pressed to his heart, his toothless mouth hanging open. 'So many paupers, Pagan – I had no idea . . .'

'They mightn't all be paupers. Not *real* paupers.' (What's that fellow doing? Peeling off from the crowd, following the

hunchback. I don't like his face.) 'Hey, you!' (Yes, you.) 'Where do you think you're going?'

Who, me? An expression of injured innocence. You're not fooling anyone, cesshead.

'Try stealing that old man's ransom, my friend, and you'll find yourself nailed to the nearest piece of wood.'

'I wasn't –'

'Now get over there and wait your turn.'

Nice to have a bit of authority. Nice to have Roland around. You don't argue with a man whose comrade looks like Saint George's big brother. Not that Roland's the slightest bit interested: he's already waist deep in beggars, and heading for the door.

The crowd parts in front of him like mist in the morning sunlight. An eerie hush descends.

'Any trouble, sergeant?'

'A little, my lord.'

'Please try to be patient, good folk.' Roland lifts his voice. 'Patience and discipline are always rewarded.'

Yes, and my Aunty Eleanor was the Queen of Persia. You can almost hear it. Almost, but not quite. No one says a word as Roland proceeds through the doorway.

With his faithful squire panting at his heels.

'I don't see why they have to sit out there.' Roland sounds harassed. 'They should be brought into this courtyard.'

'Bring them in here, my lord, and they'll steal everything that isn't bolted down.'

'Oh, Pagan –'

'It's true. Believe me. I know.'

'How can you know?'

'Because I spent two years patrolling the Jewry quarter on night watch. It wasn't much fun, but it was instructive.'

First on the left, just inside the main entrance. A narrow storeroom lined with shelves. Bundles of hemp, jars of tallow, blankets, chisels, brooms, pails, hides, rope, axes, water-bags, chamber-pots, you name it. Plus a big oak chest full of money.

Gildoin and Odo are standing guard. Odo bruised and puffy, his swollen face all the colours of the rainbow: red, orange, yellow, purple. Gildoin drawn and heavy-eyed, missing a couple of teeth. Both survivors.

Father Amiel in front of them, seated. Talking to a pauper you wouldn't touch with tongs. Ingrained with dirt, crusted with sores, smells like a leper's latrine. Stay downwind of *that* one.

'But you can't have the ransom until you tell me your name.' (Amiel, wearily.) 'You do have a name, don't you?'

The pauper nods. It's a man, anyway. You can tell that much.

'Well if you have a name, then give it to me.'

'Joseph.'

'Joseph what?'

Silence. Amiel lifts his eyes to heaven.

'Where do you come from, Joseph?' Roland steps forward. 'Where is your home?'

Not a whimper. Hardly surprising, poor dungbeetle. Time to make my contribution.

'He won't have a home, my lord. Or a name or a family or anything else. He's probably a scavenger. They live off the rubbish heaps outside the city wall. We used to see them on night watch.'

All eyes swing in my direction. There's a heavy, hopeless feeling in the air.

'Well how can I mark him down in the records if he doesn't have a name?' Amiel is tired and peevish. He bites at the end of his quill. 'We can't just say "Joseph". It isn't enough.'

Roland makes an impatient movement.

'Just give him the money.'

'But –'

'Do it.'

'But how *much*? One or ten?'

Good question. Peering at the pauper. Man or boy? Roland decides to ask.

'How old are you, Joseph?'

A goggling stare. Might as well ask a puddle of mud the way to Byzantium.

'I think he's a boy.' Amiel wants to save money. 'One dinar.'

'Give him ten. Just in case.'

'But my lord –'

'Now.'

Gildoin counts the money into Amiel's hand. Amiel passes it to Joseph. Joseph stares in wonder. Probably never seen a dinar before in his life.

'Off you go, Joseph.' Roland points him to the door. 'And may God go with you.'

Shuffle, shuffle. Hobbling out on rag-bound feet. Amiel waits until Joseph has disappeared, his mouth tight with disapproval, his nose as sharp as his pen. He frowns up at Roland, his skin the colour of candle-wax.

'My lord, I must tell you that we can't do much more

for these people,' he says. 'The Temple treasury is not a bottomless pit.'

'We must do what we can.'

'Yes, but we're not responsible. The church and the city –'

'The church and the city have thousands more to look after.' Roland's voice is like cold iron. 'There are twenty thousand poor in Jerusalem. They will be sold into slavery if we don't raise the funds to buy their release.'

'My lord, I know we have a Christian duty, but the Order also has a duty to itself. There's barely enough left for our own ransoms. What with the servants, and the mercenaries, and your fifty dinars –'

'Don't trouble with my ransom. Forget about it. That's not coming out of the treasury.'

Hold on. Wait just a moment. What's happening here? Amiel opens his mouth – and shuts it again as the next pauper appears on the threshold.

A raw, ragged woman with a face like a length of torn white wool.

'We can discuss this later, Father Amiel.' Roland begins to back out. 'Just do what you can, for the present. I'll return shortly.'

One little woman and he runs for his life. You'll have to get used to them *some* time, Roland. The cloistered days are finished. Catching up in the courtyard, as he heads for the new wing. Grabbing his belt. Pulling him back.

'Wait. My lord?'

'What is it?'

His eyes, blank and blue. Looking down his nose at me. It's no good, Roland. That doesn't work any more.

'If the Order isn't paying your ransom, my lord, then who is?'

'We'll discuss it later.'

'Oh no we won't. We'll discuss it *now*.'

Can't believe I said that. But it's time to hold firm – time to talk frankly. He blinks; sighs; removes my hand. Exuding an air of weary patience.

'Pagan, you know the Rule as well as I do. No ransom is ever paid for a Templar knight.'

'But the Rule is *broken*! You said so yourself!' (Keep calm, Pagan. Take a deep breath.) 'The Rule doesn't apply, my lord. Not in these circumstances. Anyway, if it's good enough for the Grand Master –'

'Pagan. Listen to me. No, *listen*.' Laying a hand on my head. 'Fifty dinars will buy the freedom of ten women. *Ten*. Do you think I can walk out of this city with the souls of ten women on my conscience? Or fifty children? Do you think God would ever forgive me for that?'

Christ in a cream cheese sauce. 'Honestly, my lord, do you think He'll forgive *any* of us?'

'No – you don't understand. This is different.'

'Why?'

'Because my price is higher. And so are His expectations of me. I have spoken before of His blessings, Pagan. Now I see the way clear. This is the chance I have been given to repay Him for his loving kindness, without the shedding of blood –'

'Oh, grow up, for God's sake! What do you think that stuff is in *your* veins, consecrated wine? You know they'll kill you! You know they will!' (God give me patience! God give me *patience*, you stupid, stuck-up, arrogant

oyster-head!) 'I mean who the hell do you think you are, exactly? Saint Roland of the Perpetual Martyrdom? You're no saint, Roland! You might think you are, but you're not!'

'Pagan –'

'You're no saint, because saints aren't stupid! *You're* stupid! You're so stupid that you can't think ahead! You think that sacrificing your life for a bunch of scabby, snot-nosed orphans is going to save them from slavery? You're out of your mind! The instant they hit the road they'll be snapped up by every dealer this side of Damascus – because *you* won't be there to protect them! Can't you see you'll be needed on the road? No, of course you can't. Because you're too damn worried about getting your little foothold in heaven –'

'*That's enough!*'

'I mean, you're not satisfied with having the best of everything down here, are you? You've got to have a seat right next to the throne up there as well! Because you're greedy! That's what you are, you're –'

Bang-bang!

Hit the ground. What . . .? Who . . .? Try to get my eyes back into focus.

God. He must have boxed my ears.

Standing up there with his fists clenched. Face the colour of a drunkard's nose. Speechless. Shaking. Utterly, uncontrollably, frighteningly furious.

He turns on his heel and strides away across the courtyard.

For a moment there I thought he was going to kill me. Never seen anything like it in my life. God! What a look!

The saint explodes and the earth trembles.

But you're no saint, Roland. You're a stupid, childish, pompous, gullible, pig-headed, misguided foreigner and you're not going to ruin everything just because of some crazy adolescent idea.

Because I'm not going to *let* you.

Chapter 9

The Mount Sion bath-house: a den of iniquity since the dawn of time. Or at least since the birth of Jesus. They say the plumbing dates back that far. Skulking there in its shallow pit, four steps below the level of the street, with the marble slowly dropping from its facade – slab by slab – to expose the concrete and rubble beneath.

First time I've ever seen the doors shut.

Bang-bang-bang! (Open up in there.) No pedlars hanging about with their stocks of perfume and sugar-cane. No shifty-looking men in cheap clothes and expensive jewellery. No steady flow of patrons splashing in and out through clouds of scented steam.

'Open up!'

The clash of bolts, the squeak of hinges. A quivering

collection of pouches and jowls, arranged in the shape of a face.

'Who's there?' (Voice like someone filing down steel rivets.) 'What do you want?'

'I'm looking for Joscelin.'

'Joscelin?'

'On a matter of business.'

The yellow eyeball rolls heavenwards.

'He lives upstairs.'

'I know that.' Pus-features. 'I just don't know how to get up there.'

'Around the side.'

Slam! Door swings shut. (Manners? Who needs 'em?) Probably up to no good, in there. What a cesspool. Last time I crossed the threshold – when was it? On night watch. Cut throat in a private bath. Barber's knife, purse stolen, nobody heard a thing. Perfect haunt for a snake like Joscelin. Should have known he'd end up living here.

Around the side, he says. Dark, foul, and slippery underfoot. A staircase hewn into the crumbling wall. Washing strung from every available window. Oddly quiet.

But then it's oddly quiet all over Jerusalem. No battle raging. No bells ringing. No blood flowing. The markets all empty, and everything shut: foundries, tanneries, wine shops, bath-houses – you name it. Infidel patrols on every corner. Trying not to swank about too much, because it might arouse the fury of the populace. Trying to keep the peace. Searching every passer-by for concealed weapons. No arms allowed in public, damn their godforsaken souls – so now I have to catch this venomous hornet with my bare hands.

And of course the door's bolted.

Hmmm. Won't get anywhere by announcing myself. He'll probably slip out some hidden back way. Don't have the weight to push the door open. Can't use my voice; can't light a fire; can't see any accessible windows . . .

But if I were Joscelin, I'd open my door for a dog. Even if I was only going to send it about its business.

Scratch-scratch-scratch.

So it's come to this. Sitting on my haunches, scraping away at Joscelin's door with my fingernails like some kind of hungry animal.

'Who is it?' Muffled, from inside. I'd know that voice anywhere.

Scratch-scratch-scratch. Scratch-scratch-scratch-scratch-scratch.

Footsteps. Silence. He's listening at the door.

Scratch-scratch.

Clunk of the bolt. *Now! Push!*

And *in* we go! Wham! He hits the floor, squealing – his little silver knife spins across the room.

Oh no you don't, bedlouse. Stamp on his fingers.

'Ow! Ow! Ow –'

'Don't even try it.'

'Ow, get off, get off –'

'All right.' Move the foot. Drop down fast, as he turns onto his stomach. One knee on his shoulders. A handful of hair and 'Yeow!' Pulling his head back.

'No! Please!' (He thinks I'm going to cut his throat.) 'Please –'

'Relax, Joscelin. We're old friends, remember?'

The big brown eyes strain sideways in their sockets. Bulging. Astonished.

'Pagan . . .?'

'What's the matter? Did you think I was dead? Eh?' Dragging harder, until the tears well up in those oily orbs. 'No thanks to you that I'm not, you viper.'

'Help! *Help!*'

'Shut up.' Push his head down, hard, to strike the floor. A nice little clunk of bone on wood. 'I'm not going to kill you. I wouldn't risk getting myself that dirty.'

'What – what do you want?'

'Money. I want money.' The smooth texture of silk on his back: figured silk – damask – in blue, white and gold. Imported. Expensive. 'Fifty dinars, to be precise.'

'Fifty dinars!'

'Or you won't get the *chance* to buy your freedom. It just so happens I've met Saladin, and he's a man of honour. He wouldn't even think of letting you loose on the world, if he knew what I know –'

Sudden lurch as he bucks. Not a hope, Delilah. Didn't even lose my balance. All that Templar training is beginning to pay off.

'Don't make me angry, Joscelin.'

'But I don't have it! I don't have fifty dinars!' Panting like a dog in the heat. 'I barely have enough to pay my own ransom . . .'

Look around the room. It's small, low, crowded. Stacked with firewood and buckets – endless buckets. A tiny brazier. A palliasse under a heap of tangled fabric, fustian and linen and fine wool. A painted chest. A dented cooking pot. A broken sandal.

Where did all his carpets go?

'They've been bleeding me dry,' he quavers. 'I've had to sell everything . . .'

'Who have?'

'The Silver Ring. They think I can pay my dues when there's no business. How can I take money from pilgrims when there's a war on?'

'Liar.'

'It's true! See for yourself! There's only the clothes on my back, now.'

Christ in a cream cheese sauce. Could he be telling the truth? But he never tells the truth. Never.

'What's in that chest?'

'Nothing. Garbage. Take it, if you want – it isn't worth a dinar.'

'What about these clothes? They must be worth a bit.'

'You can't have my clothes!' (Shrilly.) 'They're all I have left! I'm paying my ransom with these clothes!'

'Take them off.'

'No!'

'Do you want me to take them off for you?' Tugging his hair. 'Because you won't enjoy it, I promise.'

'Ow! Ow – all right. All right . . .'

Shifting my weight, slowly. Pulling back behind a cocked fist, ready for anything. He rolls over, sits up, sneezes. No sudden moves.

'Stay there, Joscelin. Just take them off down there.'

'But –'

'Do it!'

He wriggles out of his silken surcote, dragging it over his head, folding it into a bundle, aiming it, throwing it. Whoops! Caught it. Underneath, he's wearing a blue linen tunic embroidered at the sleeves and hem. Pulling it off and – whump! Damnation! Right in my face –

Off he goes, across the floor, grabs the knife, spins around, yells, stabs, misses. Hard to his head. Crack! Knuckles hit his cheekbone. Thrown sideways, drops the knife. I'll take that.

Using the left hand: my right is killing me.

'You want your knife, Joscelin?' (Gasping.) 'Because I'll give it to you. I'll give it to you in the guts.'

'No! Don't – don't –' Tearfully. Cowering there in his breeches, his skin pulled tight over his ribs. As pale as a maggot. Arms like chicken bones. Mottled with the yellowish smears of old bruises – he always bruised easily – at Saint Joseph's he was a walking bruise . . .

Oh, hell. What am I doing here? I'm beyond this, now. This is all in the past. It's mean and low and pathetic and filthy and I don't want anything more to do with it.

'Don't flatter yourself, Joscelin. I wouldn't waste my energy. And I don't want your clothes – they smell bad.' (Ouch, my knuckles. Hope nothing's broken.) 'But I'll take this knife, maybe it's worth a few dinars.'

No reply. He's wobbling about on all fours like a newborn lamb, dazed, dishevelled. Looking down, you can see the scars on his sticky white back. Scars from Brother Benedict's wooden cane.

What a miserable creature.

'Goodbye, Joscelin. May we never meet again, in this world or the next, and may you spend all eternity with Brother Benedict in a pit full of rotten vegetable peelings.'

One more look at his pale, pointed face, with its long eyes and short nose, disappearing behind the door as it swings shut. Outside, the air seems fresher, sweeter, and the light is dazzling. Praise the Lord, who brought me up out of

a horrible pit, out of the miry clay, and set my feet upon a rock . . .

But I still don't have fifty dinars.

There's a whole crowd of people here already – most of them down on their knees. A buzz of whispers, echoing around the cavernous dome, the arches, the chapels. Sobs and moans and the occasional beating of breasts. Mosaics flickering in the light of a thousand votive candles . . . great mountains of wax . . . never seen anything like it.

All praying for a miracle, I suppose.

Just think of the number of prayers flying up to heaven, right at this very instant. Thousands. Hundreds of thousands. Hundreds of thousands from the Holy Sepulchre alone. And most of them for money, of course. It's enough to make you despair. How am I ever going to make myself heard through this lot?

First thing to do is get close to the altar. You're nearer to God, around the altar. If this fishmonger's wife would just move her fat carcass . . . There. Thank you. Now. What do I want? I want fifty dinars.

Praise ye the Lord. Bow down thine ear, O Lord, for I am poor and needy. Deal bountifully with me for the sake of my master, O Lord, who is gracious, and full of compassion, and righteous, and walketh in the law of the Lord, and I will behave myself wisely in a perfect way, and set no wicked thing before mine eyes –

'Pagan! Pagan Kidrouk!'

An urgent hiss. Spin around, peer through the gloom; it's Sigebert the Saxon.

Terrific.

'Pagan Kidrouk, what are you doing here?'

Sigh. The Lord give me strength and endurance. I'll never understand why God took the lives of men like Bonetus and Maynard and Pons, but left Sigebert here to annoy us. Unless He doesn't particularly want Sigebert up there with Him. That I can understand.

'I'm praying, Sig. What do you think I'm doing?'

'Lord Roland has been looking everywhere for you. You have to go to him right away.'

'When I'm finished.'

'No – *now*. He told me.' (Fish-eyes popping with distress.) 'He told me I had to bring you back at once.'

And I suppose you'll start bleeding at the pores, if you have to wait. God preserve us. What am I going to do? Unless . . .

'Why does he want to see me, Sig? Anything special?'

'I don't know. Please, Pagan –'

'All right, all right. I'm coming.' Perhaps Roland has changed his mind. Perhaps the force of reasoned argument . . . well, it's possible. Following Sigebert back down the nave, picking a path through the huddled worshippers. Which reminds me.

'Sigebert?'

'Yes?'

'What on earth are *you* doing here?'

'I just said. I've been looking for you.'

'In the Church of the Holy Sepulchre?'

'Well why not? Everyone else seems to be here.'

Out in the sunlight, as harsh as a hairshirt. Sigebert wasn't made for the sun. He belongs underground, in the

dark, like a pale, blind, burrowing creature. His bleached hair, his bloodless face, his oyster eyes screwed up in a squint – he looks like a ghost.

Quick march through a square full of grieving paupers.

'It's sad, isn't it?' Sigebert unburdens his sensitive soul as he shakes off a clinging beggar, a woman with a child at her breast. 'If only we had enough money, they could all be saved.'

Sigebert the Man of Great Wisdom. What would we do without his profound insight?

'Really, Sig? Is that a fact?'

'But they might be lucky, I suppose.' Drivelling on, God help us. 'Perhaps Saladin's brother will ask for another thousand, do you think? Or somebody else will...'

'Sigebert, where are you going?' (You slug-brained moron.) 'It's this way.'

'What is?'

'Headquarters, stupid!'

'Oh – we're not going there.' Scratching his armpit. Chewing his bottom lip. 'We're going to the Patriarch's palace.'

'Why?'

'Because that's where Saladin is. Come on.'

Wait just a moment. I don't understand. Whoa, there!

'What's Saladin got to do with it? Sigebert? I thought you said Lord Roland sent you?'

'Yes, but he was going to meet with Saladin, just like everyone else. Because of Saladin's brother.'

'Saladin's *brother*?'

'Oh – I don't suppose you've heard.' (The light dawns,

at last.) 'Saladin's brother asked Saladin for one thousand poor captives as a reward for his services, and then he set them free. Because he was so sorry for them.'

'You're joking.'

'No, I'm not. So now the Patriarch and Lord Balian have gone to ask Saladin if *they* can have some captives to set free. Because we can't afford all the ransoms.'

Well I'll be – whoops! And off he goes. Trotting away down Jaffa Street, knock-kneed and slope-shouldered, with everything dangling and bouncing and swinging with each footfall: his arms, hands, head, scabbard, belt-pouch, everything. 'Come on, Pagan! Hurry!' Moving west, towards the Patriarch's palace.

Yes, yes, I'm coming.

So, the Great Man does it again. Yet another grand gesture that will go down in history. Like that time years ago, when he was besieging the castle of Kerak de Chevaliers during somebody's wedding, and he wouldn't let his engines bombard the bridal suite. Saladin the Noble Infidel. The Flower of Chivalry.

I wonder if . . .? No. Maybe? It's certainly worth a try.

Eight more steps, around the corner and – behold! The Patriarch's palace. With Infidel sentries guarding the door. Two men in turbans, one of them chewing sunflower seeds. Both staring at Sigebert as if they've never seen such a freak before in their lives.

God knows, I can't blame them.

'Um . . . Lord Roland?' he quavers. 'Lord Roland wants to see us? He's inside . . .'

Totally unintelligible. The guard just stands there, chewing. Looks as though he doesn't speak Frankish.

'Templar? Tem-plar?'

Well *you* can hang about here all day chatting, Sig. I have things to do. March straight past the smaller guard, who doesn't lift so much as an eyebrow. Must be some kind of symbolic sentry – just to show everyone who's in command. The courtyard's buzzing: thick with horses, people, supplies. Cages full of chickens. Raised voices near the water trough. A powerful smell of manure. Infidels, Infidels and more Infidels.

'Lord Roland said he'd be in the council room.' Sigebert, over my shoulder. 'Do you know where that is?'

'Yes I do. It's this way.' Through the door, up the stairs, and what a rabble! What a noise! All these dark faces, oiled black hair ... chatter, chatter ... the spicy scent of them, jammed cheek to cheek, under a cloud of wine fumes mixed with the old familiar reek of urine.

'Excuse me, can I just –? Thank you ...'

Out of my way, dogbreath. Squeezing between the armoured muscles, pushing, pushing, 'scuse me everyone, making it through to the carpet. Crowds changing. Franks, women, a little boy in a bright blue tunic. Turn left. Left again. And here's the door, smothered in straining bodies. Help! Where's the guard? This is urgent.

'Pagan Kidrouk!'

Gaspard. Pouncing like a panther.

'Pagan Kidrouk, Lord Roland –'

'I know, I know. Lord Roland wants to see me.'

'Come on.'

Who are all these people? That woman, now – what's she doing here? In her white silk and pearls. She's a *lady*. And that poor old remnant – he ought to be in bed.

'What on earth is going on here? Sergeant? Who –?'

'Petitioners.'

Of course. Petitioners. Packed so tight you have to dig your way through. Inside the room there are fewer people: Saladin, Balian, Balian's squire, Saladin's brother, the Patriarch, the Master-Sergeant . . .

Roland. Looking up. Sidling across the carpet as the Lily declaims. Bending his mouth to my ear.

'Pagan.' A whisper. 'Pagan, forgive me. I'm so sorry.'

You're *what*? You're joking. No – on second thoughts, you're not joking. The flushed cheeks, the knitted brows, the pleading eyes – you're not joking at all.

This is ridiculous.

'It was a barbarous action, I had no right –'

'To hit me? Yes you did. I'm your squire. That's what I'm here for.'

'It was wrong. "He that is slow to anger is better than the mighty." I ask your forgiveness.'

Forgiveness! Don't know whether to laugh or cry. As if it *matters*, for God's sake!

'Have you changed your mind, my lord? About the ransom?'

'Pagan –'

'Well have you or haven't you?'

He straightens up, but he's not angry. His face is as soft as duckling's down.

'No,' he says. 'I haven't.'

All of a sudden the Great Man speaks. Sitting there in his modest brown burnous and his no-nonsense slippers, on

one of the Patriarch's decorated thrones, with the Patriarch's lush carpet under his feet and the Patriarch's silk cushions hugging his backside and the Patriarch in front of him, pleading like a beggar with pretty, prayerful gestures of his manicured hands.

'Very well, worthy father.' Saladin bows his celebrated head. (Seems quite taken with the Lily.) 'I grant you seven hundred captives to free as you desire.'

Hallelujah! Buzz of excitement around the room. Roland touches my cheekbone.

'Listen, Pagan. I don't require you to follow me in this. That is the last thing I want.' Gently. Quietly. 'You can stay with the Order. I'll see that you're promoted. You will make a good sergeant.'

'Oh really?' (With half an eye on the action.) 'And why should I want to stay with the Order? I'm certainly not staying if *you* go.'

'Now, Pagan. Be sensible.'

'Be sensible! That sounds good, coming from you!'

'Shhh.' Laying his finger across my mouth, as Saladin and the Patriarch exchange elaborate courtesies. 'Don't be angry with me, Pagan. Don't let your temper cripple your intelligence. You know you don't belong in city garrisons. To squander your gifts in such a way... do you think, having found you, I would let you stray down the wrong path again?'

'Well I don't see how you're going to stop me. If you're dead.'

Hah! *That's* wiped the silly, soulful look off his face. Suddenly hit by a vision of his squire running rampant through the lowest dens in Byzantium. Frowning down his nose at me.

'Pagan, for my sake, and for the sake of your own soul –'

Blah, blah, blah. Now it's Balian's turn to present his petition. But he can't do it as well as the Lily. Balian's backbone is too stiff. His voice is too harsh. Years of wooing women have left the Patriarch as supple and sweet as a river of honey.

Saladin doesn't even wait to hear the end of Balian's speech.

'Yes, of course,' he says. 'Of course, Lord Balian, you are granted this request. Five hundred captives, to free as you wish.' He raises his voice over the hearty expressions of gratitude. 'And I *hereby declare that I will liberate every aged pauper – man and woman!*'

The response is deafening. It runs from the room, out the door, down the hall, from tongue to tongue, as fast as a fire. You can hear the news setting hearts alight beyond these walls.

Saladin sits there, soaking it up. No smiles or nods, but there's something about the way he leans back – like a man who's just finished an excellent dinner. Suddenly it's all quite clear. It all makes sense. This is what he wants: this particular feeling. Praise and awe and honour, and the blessing of his religion. A name revered throughout the world.

Well, if it's reverence you want, O Worshipful One, you can certainly have mine. You can have the lot. A mention in every prayer, a votive candle at Michaelmas, a space on my tombstone . . . anything. If you'll just grant me one favour.

'Lord Sultan!'

Pushing forward to catch his eye. Roland grabs – and

misses. (Too slow off the mark.) 'Pagan! *Pagan!*' Snatching at my collar as I hit the floor, just three steps away from the Great Man's right foot. Grovel, cringe, bow.

'By your mercy, Lord Sultan!'

Palms sweating; mouth dry; heart pounding like a drum in my ears. Saladin looks down, startled.

'What is it, boy?'

'*Pagan! Get back here! Pagan –*'

Whoops! Here he comes! If I can just get a grip on the Great Man's ankle . . . 'Your mercy, my lord! Your gracious charity! Please, my lord –'

'Wait.' Saladin's voice, like a whiplash. 'One moment, Lord Roland.'

'My lord –'

'*One moment*, Lord Roland. I wish to hear what this boy has to say.'

Roland freezes. He's going to kill me. His face is as white as new milk.

Saladin waves a careless hand at his bodyguards. (I didn't even see them closing in.)

'Well, boy?' Crisply. 'What is your name?'

'Pagan Kidrouk, my lord Sultan, and I beg –'

'Is that your father's name?'

(Is that my *what?*)

'Uh – no, my lord, it's – I'm an orphan.'

'Truly? And a Christian?'

'Yes, my lord.'

What on earth is going on here? He squints at me, frowning, his hand on his chin.

'You remind me of someone . . . no matter. Proceed. You have a request?'

'My lord, you have granted so many destitute captives their freedom –'

'And you want me to grant you your own.'

'Oh no, my lord!' (Calm down, Pagan. Calm down. *Concentrate.* Look him right in the eye.) 'It's not my freedom I want – it's my master's.'

A muffled noise behind me. Sound of Roland's teeth splintering? Hurry, hurry, or he's going to explode.

'Your master's?' The Great Man blinks. Glancing at Roland, at me, at Roland. 'Are you saying –'

'Lord Roland is my master, and he won't let the Order pay his ransom. He says fifty dinars is too much. He says he won't take so big a sum from the Temple treasury when there are women and children still to be saved. He says he can't live with the souls of fifty children on his conscience, my lord, and he won't lift a finger to save himself! Please, my lord, I know he's a knight of the Temple but he's so *good*, my lord, he's a man of honour and mercy just like you, and he's never done a cruel or ungenerous thing in his life but he still thinks he has to *atone* or something –'

'*Pagan!*'

'– I don't know why, it's crazy, he's spent his whole life trying to do the right thing and I'd pay the money myself if I had it, but I've got nothing, nothing, not even my own clothes –' (Oh please, *please*, how can I explain? You've got to. I can't bear it. If he dies . . . I can't bear it . . . what shall I *do?*)

'Hush. Quiet, now. Enough. I understand what it is you are asking.'

A long, long pause – and everything around me

dissolves in a wash of tears. Wiping them away (just pull yourself together, will you?) for a close look at Saladin. Brown face. Hollow cheeks. Cloudy eyes, fixed on Roland. Hard to tell what he's thinking. Please. Please, God, make him say yes and I'll never drink or steal or lie or swear or gamble ever again.

'Have you anything to add, Lord Roland?'

Help. Don't turn around. You might see his face.

'My lord Sultan...' A voice so harsh it sounds as if he's grinding gravel between his teeth. 'I'm sorry for this imposition on your time and patience. It was not my doing.'

'I see.'

The whole room, wrapped in silence. Everyone waiting... waiting... please, God. Please. Holding my breath as the Great Man ponders.

At last he bends his eyes to my face once more.

'Your master is an enemy of the faith,' he declares, 'but Allah honours those who honour widows and orphans. Very well. I will grant you this request.'

He seems a long way off. Buzzing in my ears... What did he say? Did he say – he said yes? I couldn't... yes. He said yes. He said *yes*! Oh God. Thank you. Thank you, God.

'Thank you, Lord Saladin.' Roland. Somewhere above my head. 'May peace be upon you for your mercy and kindness.'

Saladin nods. Roland bows. May peace be upon you... praise ye the Lord! Praise ye the Lord and all His angels! Praise Him with the sound of trumpets! Praise ye – whoops!

And hauled to my feet.

'Thank you! Thank you, my lord Sultan!' Shouting back over the heads of the audience. (Where are we going? Roland? Let go. You're hurting my arm.) 'May peace be upon you, my lord! May peace be upon you!'

Last glimpse of the Great Man. May the grace of our Lord Jesus Christ be upon our noble enemy. I don't care *what* he's done. As far as I'm concerned, he's the lost sheep in the wilderness.

The crowds part at the door to let us through. Roland still clutching my elbow.

'My lord? Don't be angry – please – my lord?'

No reply. God, he's going to kill me. But I don't care. I don't care. As long as he doesn't kill himself.

Through another door, and into another room. A small room. A library? The walls are lined with scrolls and books. He's trying to control his breathing. Drops my arm the way you'd drop a live ember.

Stands there with his hands on his hips. Chest heaving.

'Well?' he says.

'Well what?'

'How *dare* you disobey me!'

'I'm sorry, but I had to.'

'The *insult!*'

'I'm sorry.'

'You deserve to be flogged for such insolence!'

'Oh don't say that. It was only fair.'

'What?'

'Well how many times have you saved *my* life?'

Pause. He's speechless. Throws up his hands, turns on his heel, paces to the window and back again. Takes a

deep breath. Lets it out slowly. Seems to be calming down a bit.

'You shouldn't have done that, Pagan. I know you meant well, but you shouldn't have done that. It was a great shame to me. You must promise never to do anything like it ever again.'

'I'm sorry, but I can't.'

'*Pagan* –'

'My lord, how can I?' Look at me, Roland. *Look* at me. I might be your squire, but I'm also your friend. Can't you see that? Can't you see what I'm feeling? 'My lord, have some mercy. For God's sake, think of *me*. Don't you understand? You're all I have left.'

Outside, the babble of a foreign tongue, as foreign soldiers make themselves at home.

Chapter 10

Praise God for a full moon, so bright you could almost read by it. A fu'll moon makes things so much safer. You don't get lions or wolves or brigands sneaking into the camp unnoticed, under a full moon.

And here comes Roland, back from the burial. At this rate there won't be any convoy left, by the time we find a haven. If only they'd given us a bit of extra food at Tyre...

'Fig, my lord? They're not very good.'

'Where did these come from?'

'That hairy soapmaker found a grove just over the hill.'

Somewhere down the line a baby begins to scream. (Amazing it still has the energy.) Not much of a mouthful, these figs. Dry, stringy, tasteless.

Spitting the stalks into the fire.

'My lord?'

'Mmmm?'

'Even if we reach Tripoli tomorrow . . .'

'We seem to be quite close, Pagan.'

'Yes, but will they take us in? They must be overcrowded in Tripoli, as well.'

A sigh. Poor Roland. He's so weary.

'We can only hope. And pray.'

'If we don't find somewhere soon, we might have to spend the whole winter here. There aren't many ships on the sea routes, in winter.'

'God's will be done. Our first duty is to the refugees.'

Duty, duty, duty. If it wasn't for this feeble mob we'd be on our way to France by now. Tyre would have welcomed us with open arms – two healthy fighting men – and we could have sailed to Sicily with the Archbishop. Gone to seek help from the courts of Europe. Gone to rally the Order's western branches. Gone to see the *Pope*, perhaps!

Instead of which we sit here in the dust eating dross for our dinner, with half the population of Jerusalem starving to death around us.

Ah, well. Could be worse, I suppose.

'My lord?'

'Yes?'

'Is it cold in your country?'

'Not too much colder than here. My father's lands are quite far south.'

'And still you don't have baths?'

'It's not the custom.'

There are countries in the north where the ice only

melts for three days of the year. I've heard of them. But I wouldn't want to visit.

'My lord?'

'What?'

'Do they speak the same language in your country?'

'More or less.'

'What about the food? Do they eat the same food?'

'I suppose so. Basically the same. They just put it together differently.'

'And – the people?'

'What about them?'

'Do they look the same as you?'

A puzzled stare across the flames.

'Of course not. How could they? Half of them are women.'

'Yes, but – well – do they look anything like *me*?'

Pause. He's smiling. You can see the glint of teeth through his beard.

'How could they, Pagan? There's no one like you.'

'No, but I mean – are any of them as *dark* as me? As dark as a Turk? I was just thinking . . . you know . . .'

'No I don't know. Are you afraid they will stare? Then you should conduct yourself with more decorum.' He shakes his head, still smiling. 'Don't worry, Pagan. Whatever happens, you'll be all right. I promise.'

And the sparks fly up as the embers release them, fading into the shadows of dusk.

186

BUSSELTON SENIOR HIGH SCHOOL

LIBRARY

The author would like to thank John O. Ward for his assistance.

First published in 1992
This edition published in 2007

Copyright © Catherine Jinks, 1992

All rights reserved. No part of this book may be reproduced or transmitted in
any form or by any means, electronic or mechanical, including photocopying,
recording or by any information storage and retrieval system, without prior
permission in writing from the publisher. The *Australian Copyright Act 1968*
(the Act) allows a maximum of one chapter or ten per cent of this book, whichever
is the greater, to be photocopied by any educational institution for its educational
purposes provided that the educational institution (or body that administers it) has
given a remuneration notice to Copyright Agency Limited (CAL) under the Act.

Allen & Unwin
83 Alexander St
Crows Nest NSW 2065
Australia
Phone: (61 2) 8425 0100
Fax: (61 2) 9906 2218
Email: info@allenandunwin.com
Web: www.allenandunwin.com

National Library of Australia
Cataloguing-in-Publication entry:

>   Jinks, Catherine, 1963- .
>   Pagan's crusade.
>
>   For ages 12 and over.
>   ISBN 978 1 74175 231 1 (pbk.).
>
>   1. Orphans – Juvenile fiction. 2. Crusades – Third,
>   1189-1192 – Juvenile fiction. 3. Knights and knighthood –
>   Juvenile fiction. 4. Jersualem – History – Latin Kingdom,
>   1099-1244 – Juvenile fiction. I. Title. (Series : Jinks,
>   Catherine, 1963– Pagan chronicles ; 1).

A823.3

Cover & Text Design by Zoë Sadokierski
Set in Celestia Antiqua 11.5/15pt by Midland Typesetters
Printed and bound in Australia by the SOS Print + Media Group.

10 9 8 7 6 5 4 3 2

MIX
Paper from
responsible sources
FSC® C011217
www.fsc.org

The paper in this book is FSC certified.
FSC promotes environmentally responsible,
socially beneficial and economically viable
management of the world's forests.

JUNIOR HIGH SCHOOL
X   081. 01
F
JIN
LIBRARY

Pagan's Crusade

The Pagan Chronicles

Book One

Catherine JINKS

ALLEN & UNWIN

CATHERINE JINKS is a scholar of medieval history and a prolific author for teenagers, children and adults. Her books have been published to wide acclaim in Australia and overseas and have won numerous awards. She loves reading, history, films, TV and gossip, and says she could write for eight hours straight every day if she had the chance. Catherine lives in the Blue Mountains of NSW with her husband and daughter.

www.catherinejinks.com

THE PAGAN CHRONICLES

Pagan's Crusade
(shortlisted CBCA and Victorian Premier's Literary awards)

Pagan in Exile

Pagan's Vows
(winner CBCA Book of the Year Award for older readers)

Pagan's Scribe
(winner Victorian Premier's Literary Award for children's literature)

Pagan's Daughter
(notable book CBCA Book of the Year Award for older readers)

The Pagan Chronicles

'Full of the richly-textured, high-smelling, highly individualistic atmosphere of the Middle Ages, Catherine Jinks's Pagan series offers unforgettable characters in an extraordinary setting and time, presented in crisp, pungent prose.'

SOPHIE MASSON

'Humour, romance, adventure, violence – who would have thought Medieval Jerusalem could be so much fun?'

LILI WILKINSON

'The Pagan Chronicles are a kind of medieval version of Tin Tin, meticulously researched and told with a delightfully slapstick, cinematographic vigour.'

URSULA DUBOSARSKY

'What a romp! Not since Don Quixote took up with Sancho Panza has a knight had a squire like Pagan Kidrouk.'

Voice of Youth Advocates

'There have been few characters in recent historical fiction more vibrant than the street-smart, fast-talking protagonist of this series.'

School Library Journal

'Rich, vivid storytelling, with a sturdy base in historical events, and undercurrents both comic and serious.'

Kirkus Reviews (STARRED REVIEW)

'Jinks dramatically evokes a historical time that was particularly dark and dirty ... Along with the drama and darkness, readers will find intensity and, yes, humor. Series fans may find other books set in the Middle Ages pallid after this one.'

AMERICAN LIBRARY ASSOCIATION

'Pagan is a real, live boy who leaps off the page and compels you to listen to his story.'

KIRSTY MURRAY

'Humour? Rage? Agony? Spiritual journeys? Murder? Moral turpitude? Twists both welcome and dismaying? This decidedly unique historical saga has it all.'

Kirkus Reviews (STARRED REVIEW)

'Brimming with wit and fascinating details of medieval history, with its vividly drawn characters ... this emotionally satisfying epic brings the Middle Ages to life.'

The Horn Book